BT

D1145182

Four Aces

Millions of dollars of silver had been extracted from the mines around Tombstone, so Crazy Ned Edwards was in seventh heaven when he hit a seam worth a fortune further south at River Bend. However, saloon-keeper Lance Patterson had envious eyes on the mine and was planning murder and mayhem.

Matters got worse when Lance hired the notorious Clanton clan and the only other hope was Marshal Wyatt Earp. However he was a hundred miles away so it all looked grim indeed.

Now bullets begin to fly and the robbers seem destined to win. Or does Lady Luck have another ace up her sleeve?

By the same author

The Mustang Hunters

Four Aces

Jack McCleod

A Black Horse Western

ROBERT HALE · LONDON

© Jack McCleod 2005
First published in Great Britain 2005

ISBN 0 7090 7849 8

Robert Hale Limited
Clerkenwell House
Clerkenwell Green
London EC1R 0HT

Typeset by
Derek Doyle & Associates, Shaw Heath.
Printed and bound in Great Britain by
Antony Rowe Limited, Wiltshire.

ONE

The two horsemen were in a jovial mood as they guided their mounts down the lower slopes of the towering 2,500 foot Miller Peak. The worst of the long grinding journey out of Mexico across the border into Arizona was behind them.

'We should be in Bisbee before nightfall,' Tim Roberts called as he leaned on the pommel of his powerful cream and chestnut quarter horse. 'Am I looking forward to a decent American meal, steak and fries and real bread. You betcha! Not red-hot chillis and tough tortillas with everything. Maybe a taste of real whiskey, too.'

'Whass the matter, *amigo*, don' you like tequila? It too fiery for you?' His companion was a Mexican, a wide-brimmed sombrero shielding his cheerful face from the blazing heat of the sun, his lithe body adorned in tight-waisted velveteens, embroidered and gaudily encrusted with buttons of pearl. 'For me iss the Yankee *muchachas* I look forward to see.'

'Yeah? Well, you got a one-track mind, ain't you? You shoulda been a sailor. A gal in every port.' Roberts reined in, whipped off his low-crowned grey Stetson to run a gloved hand through his mop of tousled curls, as a bead of sweat trickled down his temple. 'Me, I'm just glad we got up through that canyon without Brandy breaking a leg. Them rocks were as sharp as knives.'

'*Sí.*' Chico Chavez sat his black mustang and peered across the vista of contorted rocks scattered haphazardly as if by the throw of some ancient god. 'Such a great stretch of nothingness. How the hell the Apache ever manage to live here beats me.'

Tim was attired in faded and creased denim jacket and jeans, with more the look of an easy-going cowhand. 'I guess we should thank our lucky stars Geronimo and his boys are cooling their heels in a Florida dungeon,' he muttered, 'or we wouldn't be—'

His words were cut off by the snap of a rifle shot and his natural reaction was to duck his head and pull his horse around for cover. 'Where'd that come from?' he yelled. 'Somebody taking a pot at us?'

'If they are they have mighty poor aim,' Chico cried as two more shots cracked out. He stood in the stirrups and looked about. 'Maybe it somebody out hunting?'

'No. There's somebody down there. He's kinda

waving at us. Maybe he's in trouble.'

'Less go find out,' Chico yelled, and gave a touch of his vicious spurs to his mustang, Satan, sending him spurting away.

Tim Roberts jammed his hat back on his head, drew one of his twin long-barrelled Colts, and set off in his wake, weaving the quarter horse through the rocks until they reached a winding ribbon of a narrow trail.

A white-bearded old guy in a battered hat and dusty clothes was standing before a two-horse wagon holding a lever-type Ballard rifle, his finger on the trigger but barrel aimed at the sky. 'I saw you two up on the ridge and thought you were going to pass on by,' he wheezed, huskily. 'I could do with some help here.'

'Lost a wheel, eh, old-timer?' Tim replied, holstering the Peacemaker and swinging down. 'Lucky for you we were passing, huh? You coulda been stranded out here in the desert.'

'Aw, I wouldn't'a been stranded. I was just thinkin' of unharnessing the nags and riding 'em in. See that pole I carry? Tried leverin' up the bed, but the dang thang snapped like a dry twig. Near trapped my leg. If you two could. . . ?'

'Sure.' Tim grabbed hold of the back of the wagon bed and braced himself. 'Come on, *amigo*, show us your strength. One, two, *three*!'

Together the two travellers hefted up the heavy buckboard. 'C'mon, gramps, quick with that wheel,' the Mexican said, as his veins bulged and beads of sweat burst out on his brow. 'We can't stand here all day.'

'Got it. Now all I need's another cotter pin. Hand me that wrench, boys.'

'You oughta keep them wheels greased better,' Tim told him as the wagon was once more ready to move.

'Aw, I ain't got time for thangs like that. I'm too dang busy.' His weatherbeaten face creased into a hundred wrinkles as he appraised them. 'I got a small farm ten miles down the trail at the source of the San Pedro. But I don't bother running cows no more. Just got a plot of corn, thassal.'

'So, how come,' Chico asked, 'you so busy?'

'Ned Edwards.' The old man offered his hand to Tim, avoiding the question. 'Sure was surprised to see you two. Where you come from?'

'Oh, we've been down to Santa Cruz for the fiesta,' Chico explained grabbing Ned's paw, too, to shake it vigorously. 'Tim's horse here, she real fast. She go like a ball from a cannon – whoom! He pick up plenty prize money.'

'Yeah, which you spend even faster on fancy women. Now we ain't so well off I guess we'll be looking for work as cowhands or wranglers along the San Pedro.'

'You came through Skeleton Canyon?'

'You said it, meester. Thass the only sign we had

of man or beast, bones bleached by the sun and wind.'

Tim grinned. 'Lucky we didn't leave ours there, too. I was told it was a short cut, but it was a damned hard one.'

'That's the old smugglers' trail,' Ned remarked, stuffing a pipe with tobacco and lighting up. 'Apaches used it, too.'

He puffed and beamed a bit at them. 'You boys, you seem nice friendly fellas. Not like some of the riff-raff you bump into around here. Frontier scum most of 'em; would cut your throat for a quarter.'

'Yeah,' Tim said, 'we've met a few.'

'Look, howdja like to work for me? I'm bustin' to tell somebody so I'm tellin' you. I've got a mine back up in the hills. I been working this area for years. Crazy Ned they call me. But how wrong could those coyotes be? Boys, I've struck it rich.'

He suddenly began to do a wild kind of high-land fling in the middle of the trail, waving his hat about and screaming at them. '*Rich*, boys! They won't call me crazy now.'

Chico pushed back his sombrero, his dark eyes gleaming, curiously. 'How rich?'

Ned stood panting as he ceased his wild dance. He fished in his pocket and produced a small silver nugget, brandishing it at them. 'Boys, that's for you for helping me. There's more where that comes from. I like you two. I judge a man on first aquaintance and my instinct says you ain't like most of the varmints round here.'

Tim took the proffered nugget, his cheek dimpling into a grin as he examined it. 'It sure is heavy. Looks like real silver to me. But we don't want this. You don't owe us—'

'Sure we do,' said Chico. 'Don't forget, *amigo*, we got to eat today.'

'Go on, take it.' Ned slapped his fist into his hand. 'Boys, I got a proposition. I need help to work this vein. You come in with me. Be my partners. And we'll split everything we get. It's my mine but I cain't say fairer than that.'

Tim gave a whistle of awe as he tucked the nugget into his shirt pocket. 'Maybe we'll take you up on that, Mr Edwards.'

'Oh, no, *amigo*.' Chico shook his head, vehemently. 'Not me. I got a weak back. I no go diggin' down dark holes. This is Crazy Ned; you not gonna be fooled by him, huh?'

'It's you'll be crazy iffen you turn me down. But suit yourselves.' Ned scowled at them, tugging at his beard. He glanced up at the sun in the haze of sky. 'It's past high noon. I gotta be going. I'm supposed to meet my niece in River Bend. She's arriving on the stage from Tombstone. I'm gonna be dang well late.'

He knocked out his pipe and climbed up on to the wagon, grabbing the reins. 'Yeah, she thinks I'm a crazy old desert rat, too. Wants me to go back to Tombstone and take it easy in a rocking chair the rest of my natural years. Not now. Not no way. I ain't the retirin' sort.'

'Listen, old-timer, if you've really got a big find you didn't oughta go shouting your mouth off about it to all and sundry,' Tim advised, swinging back on to Brandy. 'At least, not until you get your claim properly registered. There's one hell of a lot of ruthless claim-jumpers about.'

'Don't worry, youngster. Mum's the word. Hey, look, River Bend's ten miles on past my place. You'll be there way before me. Could you do me another favour, tell my niece I been delayed but I'm on my way?'

'What's she look like? What's her name?'

'Lucy. You cain't miss her. She's a purty li'l thang.'

'*Señor*' – Chico swept off his sombrero and flashed a smile – 'I am always ready to help a lady in distress.'

'And, boys,' Ned hollered, as they cantered away, 'think over my offer. You won't get a better in this life.'

River Bend was a pleasant small township, its wide main street shaded by graceful cottonwoods, ample water drawn by windpumps from the nearby stream, which widened out further along the valley to stimulate the growth of grama grass and provide good grazing for cattle. Naturally, would-be ranchers had made claims to this strip, hanging fast in the face of vicious Apache attacks. But now in the 1880s a certain peace and prosperity had come to the area. The ranchers found a ready market for their beeves in the tumultuous bonanza town of Tombstone where already millions of dollars' worth of silver had been dug from the ground.

River Bend was far from tumultuous, just a scattering of stores, an eatery, blacksmith's, meat mart, billiards hall, a couple of saloons and barber shop to service the needs of the settlers.

Tim and Chico cantered in, watered their horses and hitched them to a rail as Tim spotted an assayer's office. A few hopeful prospectors, disappointed by their efforts in Tombstone, had moved to the town to try their luck in the hills to the north. They had come across small outcrops of silver but so far none had struck it big.

'Hey,' Tim said, 'let's go see how much this nugget is worth.'

Chico, however, was more interested in a gaudily attired lady, an absurd hat on her head, an ostrich-feather boa around her throat, and her knees hobbled by a tight dress, its silk flounces swishing around her ankles, who was strolling by on the canopied sidewalk.

'Hey, *señorita*,' he called to her, 'you know you got a birdie sittin' on your head?'

'As long as that's all it's doing, darling.' She smiled painted lips at him lazily and swayed on her

12

way like a gaudy galleon in full sail, her bustle waggling.

'Look, *hombre*, she wearin' one of them new-fangled ass-coolers. Ain't she a sight for sore eyes? Wait for me, lady.'

Tim caught him by the scruff of the neck as he started to follow and hauled him back. They watched the 'lady' push through the batwing doors of the town's biggest two-storey saloon, the Silver Cartwheel, from which the tinkle of an ill-tuned piano wafted.

'If she's gone in there she ain't no lady. And if you want to make her acquaintance she'll be expecting you to pay for the privilege, so come on.'

Tim hauled his pal towards the assay office which bore the sign, 'Gold and Silver bought. Fair prices.' Once inside they saw a wiry-haired man of middle years. He had a neatly trimmed spade beard, and wore an eye-shade and apron. He was poking with iron tongs at some kind of metal he was heating in a fierce forge.

He looked up, put the tongs aside and asked, 'Yes, how can I help you gents?'

'How much for this?' Tim asked, bluntly, handing him the small nugget.

REUBEN HOROVITZ, PROPRIETOR, was the name proclaimed on his board. He fixed an eyeglass and squinted at the metal. 'Not high quality,' he muttered. 'I give you ten dollars.'

Tim took a sudden distrust to the shifty way the man with the foreign accent looked at him and quickly glanced away. 'I see. In that case I think I'll hang on to it. I was told this is almost pure silver. Maybe I can find a more generous buyer.'

'Who are you?' Horovitz glanced dismissively at the slim young cowboy in his dusty range clothes. 'What you know? I have years of experience of metallurgy and I tell you this is worth fifteen dollars at the most.' He went to his till drawer, took out the cash and offered it. 'Take it or leave it.'

'We take,' Chico said, going to grab it.

'No, we leave,' Tim told him, staying his hand.

'What you do, *hombre*? That lady, 'less I hurry, she might be gone.'

'She'll be there.'

The assayer had not returned the nugget but was studying it again. 'Very well. Twenty dollars, boys.'

'Good,' Chico said.

'Not good. We gotta pay for the horses' livery tonight. I ain't leaving them out on the street. No dice, mister. Let's go.'

Tim reached out a hand for the nugget and Reuben Horovitz reluctantly handed it over. But as they opened his glass-panelled door he called out, 'OK, you drive a hard bargain. Fifty dollars. My final offer.'

'Well that sounds better,' Tim replied, exchanging the nugget for the cash in greenbacks.

The assayer held it in two fingers and eyed them, quizzically. 'Just where did you get this?'

'An old guy give it us for helping him,' Chico blurted. 'Crazy Ned they call him.'

'Let's vamoose, partner,' Tim gritted out, dragging him from the shop and shoving him up against a wall of shiplap wood. 'You got a stupid mouth sometimes, Chico.'

'Why, what I do?' the Mexican protested.

'I wish you hadn't said that. We don't want all and sundry to know about Ned's find. There'll be a stampede up there. Remember, we're gonna work for him.'

'We are?'

'Here's your share, twenty bucks. Go find your belle of the ball. Me, I'm gonna eat someplace.'

'Twenty? That not half of fifty.'

'Remember the hosses? They need their oats, too.' Tim tucked the thirty into his shirt pocket. 'Maybe we'll have to rustle up a few ol' boys for a horse race.'

'*Sí*, I'll ask around in the saloon. I'll tell them how fast is Brandy, how she whip every contender in Santa Cruz, how you even win Satan for me from that drunken *haciendado*. That why we had to leave.'

'He honoured his bet. There was nothing illegal about it.'

'Yeah, but maybe he change his mind when he sober up. Satan, he not just ordinary mustang, he part aristocrat, too.'

'Thoroughbred, you mean. Look, don't go shouting off your mouth. Just tell 'em I'm pretty hot and anybody wants to try me tomorrow, we're ready and waiting. OK?'

Tim watched his friend run off towards the Silver Cartwheel, shook his head and smiled. 'He's woman crazy, that boy.'

TWO

The roulette wheel was spinning in the Silver Cartwheel although it was only late afternoon. Lance Patterson stood on the balcony, leaning on its carved rail, and watched the proceedings down below with satisfaction. A bunch of cowboys from an outlying ranch was hunched along the mahogany bar noisily quenching their thirsts with beer and whiskey. His croupier, Poker Nell, in bustle and big hat, was raking in chips, and some Mexican in a sombrero had ensconced himself on a horsehair sofa with his arms around two of the saloon doxies, who squealed as he squeezed and fondled them.

'Things are livening up early tonight,' Lance drawled to his sidekick and chief bouncer, Buster Davis. 'Keep an eye on that Mex. Tell him he ain't allowed to squeeze the fruit unless he plans to buy.'

'Sure, boss.' Buster was a broken-nosed, thickset

pug of a man. 'He'll be one squashed fruit if he tries.'

Both men were respectably attired in dark suits, Buster with a blue bandanna around his throat, but Lance sporting clean white linen and a loose bow tie. A handsome man in a dark, hirsute way, he raised a little finger to stroke his pencil moustache in a conceited manner. 'Tell Darling Dolly to give 'em a song or two. Let's get this joint jumping.'

Darling Dolly was the stage soubriquet of the once slim but now somewhat gaunt Dolly Parsons. They had met in Kansas City when Dolly was in her prime. Tacked to the saloon wall was a big poster from that time when Dolly topped the bill at the city music hall. But now, like her, ten years later it had become faded and ragged around the edges. She had fallen for the charms of Lance, a gambling man, but when he got into one of his regular scrapes for dealing from the bottom of the pack they had drifted westwards, one town after another, until they reached River Bend. There Lance decided it was time to open his own saloon.

When Buster spoke to her, Dolly gave a shrug of her bony shoulders and slipped from her bar stool, signalled to the professor of the keyboard, who began to rattle out their rehearsed version of 'With Cat-like Tread. . . .' *Pirates of Penzance* had been a big hit in New York four years before and this was a pirated copy. In her ankle-length, off-the-shoulder, scarlet satin dress, Dolly began to tiptoe among the tables in her high-heeled slippers, flinging her gaunt arms about in an extremely exaggerated fashion. Her voice was hoarse as she sang, her face tense beneath its flour-paste paleness, her lips and cheeks rouged, her blue eyes darkly outlined by kohl beneath a fringe of hennaed hair.

She's getting past it, Lance thought, as he watched her. She had hit the big Four-0 the year before. Their hot romance had fizzled out and they only occasionally tried to fan its flames these days. Maybe it was time to get rid of her. All those theatrical gesticulations; it made her look ridiculous. However, he was uneasily aware that Dolly still had a kind of razor-sharp sexuality that attracted the clientele. Apart from that she more or less ran the joint for him, ordering liquor and supplies, helping behind the bar when business hotted up, keeping an eye on their Chinese cook, and stepping in to quell any catfights between his calico queens.

Lance had purchased six of the latter to entertain the punters. A mixed bunch, no accounting for men's taste, for variety was the spice of life! There was the Japanese girl, Flower, who had been shipped to San Francisco in a crate, used as the whore of a railroad gang and sold on to him for twenty bucks. Black Bess was the daughter of a former slave who had emigrated west after the war. Peruvian Paula had also ended up among the fron-

tier flotsam. That Mexican free-loader currently
had his arms around both her and the foul-
mouthed, grossly fat Virginia. She had been the
mail-order bride of a settler who had been slaugh-
tered by Apache as she cowered in the cellar. She
had been a little odd ever since. There was the
Mex woman, Maria, who gave him no trouble, and
his latest, luscious recruit, French Fanny, a young
girl whose parents had been killed in a stage-coach
robbery. Lance had seduced her and added her to
his team. It was easy money. Most of their earnings
went into his pocket. If they argued, Buster
roughed them up. Sometimes, when it was
cowboy's pay night Lance persuaded Dolly to help
them out.

Over in one corner was his gang of toughs playing a desultory game of poker. The four Rs: Raker,
Rafe, Randall and Rusty. Buster had persuaded
him he needed protection. They were the best he
could recruit at a reasonable rate. Lance had
thrown in the inducement of a daily free bottle of
whiskey. They were his biggest outlay. So far they
had been useful by stepping in when card games
turned violent, or by tossing out troublemakers
like that Mexican – why didn't Buster do something about him? Lance kept them on the payroll
because he had aspirations to extend his opera-
tions: lend money at exorbitant rates; buy up land;
become a man to be reckoned with in the commu-
nity. Their back-up might come in handy.

Dolly had progressed to her version of *Climbing Over Rocky Mountain*, strolling through the tables, running her fingers through one man's greasy hair, sitting on the knee of another, moving on, stroking her velvet-gloved finger across the cheek of some beaming old-timer. It was hand-me-down trickery, but it worked. Lance Patterson, himself, had to admit that. She was a game old hustler.

A commotion broke out over on the couch. Buster had hauled the over-amorous Mexican to his feet by his frilled shirtfront and shoved him towards the bar. 'If you wanna enjoy the facilities of the house go spend some dough, pal.'

His big hat dangling on his back, his silver rowels jangling, his black hair hanging over his brow, Chico shrugged his shoulders, haughtily, let forth a string of Spanish curses, and said to the barman, 'How you like that that guy manhandling me? If I weren't—'

'What's your poison, greaser?' the 'keep snapped. 'We don't like troublemakers from south of the border. Savvy?'

'Sure I savvy.' Chico peeled off a greenback and tossed it down. 'Geev me tequila and a beer. *Savvy?*'

Dolly had finished her song and strolled over to chat to Patterson. 'Hey, sweetheart, you seeng like a nightingale.' Chico slipped an arm around her slim waist, hugged her into him, stared into her watery blue eyes and crooned, 'How about you

21

geev me a leetle kiss?'

'Cool down, hot pants,' Dolly drawled. 'It's only five in the afternoon. There's a long night to go.'

'When I look at you and hear you sing I know no knowledge of time.' Chico pursed his lips close to hers. 'Suddenly my heart it beats fast.'

'Sure and I bet it ain't the only thang that's beating,' Dolly said. 'You're quite a cutie, aincha?'

'Hey, greaser,' the 'keep spat out. 'You been warned once. Keep your hands off the merchandise unless—'

'Unless I pay? But how could I pay for such a beautiful one? I would need a king's ransom.'

'You're a real flatterer, aincha?' Dolly said, but, even knowing that it was just a tease, she felt her knees going weak and her senses spinning like she was some young girl. 'Listen,' she whispered, putting her lips close to his ear, 'you don't have to pay. The others are work. You will be playtime. Don't get too drunk. Come around about eight. I'll be upstairs in the office.'

'*Sí, señorita*, I am your slave.' Chico whooped with glee, took a slug of the tequila and shouted out a challenge. 'Any of you *hombres* think you got a fast pony? You wouldn't have a chance of beating my *amigo's*. He beat every horse in Mexico.'

The boast was all but true. They had done well at Santa Cruz. The quarter horse was a copper-bottomed sure bet. A muscular, bulldog type, with well-rounded hind-quarters and a deep heart,

Brandy possessed a terrific acceleration which made her ideal both for cutting cows out of a herd and on the race course.

'None of you could touch that mare. See, she's hitched outside.' Chico pointed through the window. 'Is she not a beauty? She blasts out of the start like bullet from gun. She don' draw a breath 'til she past the finish line.'

The cowpokes turned to stare at the Mexican, indignantly. 'She wouldn't smell my Smoky,' one yelled. 'He's like greased lightning.'

'Hold it!' Lance shouted, raising his hand for quiet. 'Just how much you willing to put on the nose of that nag of yours?'

'One hundred dollars, 'Chico announced, proudly. 'She not mine. She my friend's.'

'Well, you better go tell your friend to have her ready in half an hour,' Lance cried. 'I'm gonna hold you to that bet. What's more I'll put up a fifty-dollar prize for the winner.'

'You got a bet, fella.' Chico reached out his arm to shake with Lance. 'I go get my friend ready.'

'Yeah, you do that, pal.' Patterson went along to the cowboy with the horse called Smoky. 'OK, Danny?' He gave him a wink. 'You know what to do?'

'Sure. The usual treatment.' The tough, wiry little cowpoke gave him a twisted grin. 'He won't have a hope in hell. We'll make mincemeat of him.'

*

Corned beef hash was what Tim Roberts was enjoying along at a restaurant simply labelled Eats. He had soaked in a hot tub after a shave at the barbershop, and, all in all, was glad to be back in the good old US of A. He was persuaded to take a brandy in his coffee, and leaned back in his chair after the repast, putting up his boots. It was good to relax. What did they say in Mexico? A man with a full stomach was *mucho contento*. Of course, in these parts flies were a present guest at the feast in spite of the efforts of a small boy who was paid to go round flapping at them with a fan. 'At least they're better fed flies up here than down south of the border,' Tim quipped, as he tipped him a dime.

There was the warning halloo of a trumpet and a four-horse stage came clattering along the street, flashing past the window. The Tombstone to Bisbee line making a detour to drop off mail and a passenger at River Bend.

He hurried off down the street in time to see a young woman retrieving her travelling bag from the stage boot. She was dressed plainly in a brown, tight-waisted costume. She might be slim but, as she bent over, Tim could tell *she* had no need of a bustle. She seemed nicely appointed both aft and fore beneath all those clothes. She had a lady's stiff-brimmed Stetson on her head, from the back

24

of which her fawn hair hung down in a kind of loose bun.

'Miss Lucy?' he enquired.

She turned to face him, her frank, bright-violet eyes regarding him from an intelligent face innocent of rouge and powder. Old-fashioned soap and water was good enough for her complexion. 'Do I know you?'

'Nope. I – uh—' Tim stuttered. 'Your uncle, Ned Edwards, he asked me to meet you. He's been delayed. He'll be along soon.'

'So how do you know me.'

'Waal, he said you'd be the prettiest li'l gal north of the border. So, that seems clear to me.'

'Pretty? You think so?'

'I sure do.'

'In that case,' she said, as the stage moved away, 'maybe you could help me with my bag.'

'Sure, I'll stick it up here in the shade of the sidewalk out of the way while we wait for him.'

'How do you know my uncle?'

'Oh, I met him this afternoon. You fancy a drink or a coffee or something?' He noticed her looking across at the Silver Cartwheel from which a lot of noise was emanating. 'No, I don't mean in there. It . . . er . . . it ain't respectable. There's a restaurant up the road.'

'You mean it's a cathouse? Don't worry, I'm well aware of the world's wicked ways. There's about fifty of them and a hundred saloons in Tombstone.

But, of course we've got a population of thirty thousand now. A lot of men but very few women.'

'You don't say. That's very interesting.' Tim sat on the sidewalk and she sat beside him. 'So what do you do, Lucy?'

'Well, I certainly don't work in a cathouse.'

A blush rose to Tim's cheeks.'I – uh – I didn't mean to imply any such thing. I—'

She smiled at him, curiously. 'I work in my father's emporium. We sell everything from needles to buggies. I'm chief cashier. He was one of the first traders to arrive in Tombstone and he's done well for himself. We come of an industrious family. My father has, thanks to God, no time for idlers and drunkards. So, Mr er. . . ?'

'Roberts. Tim Roberts.' He pulled off his glove and offered his hand, and was surprised how soft and cool was hers. 'I suppose I ought to say I like a drink but I'm certainly no drunkard, and I work hard if I need to, but I'm not a man of any great wealth. My family never had none and I, well, I guess I've just drifted around north and south of the line.'

'A drifter, eh? Well,' she sighed, 'there's a lot around.'

Just then Chico came dashing out of the Silver Cartwheel and across the street to them, waving his arms, excitedly. 'Tim, we've got a race on. We make one hundred and feefty dollars, *amigo*.'

'What?' Tim jumped to his feet. 'What you talking about?'

26

'The saloon-keeper he put up feefty dollar prize and I bet him a hundred dollar we win.'

'A hundred? We haven't got a hundred dollars between us, you idiot. How we gonna pay him if we lose?'

'We ain't gonna lose.'

'Oh, no? We just rode across the mountains from Mexico. Brandy's tuckered out. Me, too. I've just had a big meal and a brandy. All I want is to find a hotel room and relax for the night. The horse should be in his stable, too. I told you to arrange a race for tomorrow.'

Tim was a young man of medium height, of athletic build, his muscles honed hard from time in the saddle, not one to pick a fight. But he grabbed Chico by his shirt and raised his fist. 'You damned fool.'

'Hey, why everybody keep grabbing at my shirt? Wass wrong, *amigo*?'

'What's wrong?' Tim saw men spilling out of the Cartwheel followed by Lance Patterson and his jockey, Danny. 'If you don't know I can't tell you.'

'Howdy,' Lance said, sticking out his paw. 'Has he told you the bet? A hundred on the nose. You ready to ride? Come on.'

Tim shrugged with despair at the girl and then spotted Ned driving his wagon down the street. 'There's your uncle. I guess this is so long.'

'You seem to have got yourself into a bit of a fix,' she smiled. 'I think we'll have to watch.'

*

Pony racing was a popular sport at River Bend and there was already a well-defined track stretching away from the starting post, down a dip through a bosky wood and back around by the river bend: a course of about a mile and a half.

'My friend's made a mistake,' Tim told Lance Patterson, who was astride his horse organizing the event. 'I'm not ready for it. I'd like to take a look at the course and do this in the morning.'

But already folks had heard of the race and were coming out from the town on horseback and in buggies to watch. 'Too bad, pal. The Mex threw down the gauntlet,' Lance sneered at him. 'You can't chicken out now.'

A dozen cowboys had decided to join in the race for the big prize and were whooping and milling about at the starting line, whipping and spurring their horses into a frenzy while at the same time hanging on to the reins to hold them back.

Tim had never seen the necessity for the whip. He calmed Brandy, his proud, magnificent horse, with his voice, walking her back and forth behind the pack. Chico, he noticed, was employing their usual tactics, sitting on Satan a hundred yards up the track.

'What's that joker doing?' Patterson demanded.

'He's not in the race,' Tim shouted back. 'He just rides along the sidelines to encourage us.'

'Yeah, well, I don't like it.' But it was too late to object. The town mayor had his flag raised as he stood on a box. Chico gave a shrill whistle. Brandy pricked up her ears and either sensed or saw her stablemate and she was off like a flash, perfect timing as the flag dropped. Chico's boast about her was not an idle one. She charged past the mob of horses and set off to catch Satan who was now galloping away on the sidelines ahead of them. 'Come on, gal,' Tim urged as he crouched low over her neck and felt the surge of power between his legs, her hoofs drumming beneath him. Maybe he could pull this off?

But the pack of horses was hot on her tail, a couple of lengths behind, and the lightweight jockey, Danny, was alongside him as they went down into the wood, looking across at him, his face a snarl as he whipped at Smoky's flanks.

They caught up and passed Chico on Satan and, suddenly, like a flash, Tim saw Danny's upraised whip hissing back at him. He tried to duck, but it cut across his cheek. The blow made him lose his concentration and, what was more, as Danny dashed on ahead, two of his cowboy comrades closed in on Tim from either side, slashing their wrist quirts at him. He had to ease up or they would have crushed his legs.

Chico came to the rescue, shouting out in anger, galloping Satan alongside the assailants and with a wild leap from the saddle caught hold of one of them and dragged him spinning along the ground.

By the time they were out of the wood Tim was well behind the mob, their dust kicked up in his face. But he wasn't done yet. He gave Brandy her head, urging her on, and went streaming around the outside to see Smoky four lengths ahead. 'Come on, sweetheart,' he gritted out. 'You can make it.' Slowly they gained on the leader, one length, two lengths, but Brandy was tiring and the winning post was in sight. The journey across the mountains had taken too much out of the mare.

He eased up on her and came in second. Chico came galloping in behind them, complaining vehemently, as the mayor prepared to present the fifty dollars to the jubilant Danny.

'I object,' Chico screamed. 'You a gang of cheats. You jump my man in the wood.' He pointed at Danny. 'Disqualify that crook. He don't win. We did.'

'What's he on about?' the portly mayor asked. 'I didn't see any cheating.'

'He's right,' Tim said. 'They forced me out of the race.' He pointed to the bleeding cut on his cheek. 'Where do you think I got this?'

'It's just sour grapes. Probably got caught by a low branch.' Lance stood beside the mayor and held out his hand expectantly. 'How about our bet? You two strangers owe me a hundred dollars. Or is it you who are the crooks?'

What was the use of arguing? The townsfolk were getting angry, one shouting out, 'Come on, pay up.' Tim pulled out all he had. 'Here's fifteen on account. How much you got, Chico?'

The Mexican made a down-turned grimace. 'Ten.'

'We'll have to give you an IOU for the rest,' Tim said, forcing Brandy through the throng to collect his gunbelt from Ned Edwards and Lucy on their wagon. 'Sorry about this,' he muttered. 'Looks like I got a bit of trouble on my hands.'

'Lock him up, Sheriff,' Lance called out. 'He ain't getting away with this.'

And a woman screeched, 'We oughta tar an' feather 'em an' run 'em out of our town.'

Ned stood up on his wagon, calming them with his hands. 'These young fellas are working for me. I'll settle up. How much they owe? Seventy-five?' He pulled a chunk of silver from his pocket and tossed it to Lance. 'That should cover it.'

A smile spread over Patterson's face as he tested the nugget with his teeth. 'Hey,' he drawled, 'this looks like the real McCoy.'

'You shouldn't have done that,' Tim said. 'But thanks, anyway, Mr Edwards.'

'Don't worry. I'll take it out of your wages. Me an' Lucy will go get a bite to eat then head back to the farm. You come out in the morning. Got enough for a room?'

'*Si*, 'Chico butted in. 'I got a couple more

31

dollars in my pocket I didn't tell them about. We'll bed down with the horses in the livery.'

Lucy smiled and waved to Tim as her uncle moved the wagon away among the folks going back to town. 'Try not to get into any more trouble.'

Tim's cheek dimpled as he shook his head. 'We'll try.'

THREE

Chico Chavez made a beeline for the backstairs of the Silver Cartwheel, according to the directions whispered to him by Darling Dolly, glancing around to make sure he was not seen. Sure enough she answered his knock and let him in to the office of Lance Patterson. It was palatially appointed for those parts with desk, armchairs, a drinks cabinet and big iron safe in the corner. 'What's your affliction, apart from wimmin?' Dolly asked, still in her off-scarlet, ankle-length sheath and velvet gloves. 'Best Frenchie Champagne?'

'That'll do me fine.' Chico clinked a glass of the bubbly stuff with hers. 'I came as fast as I could. I'm in bad trouble. I lost the bet. I got no money.'

'Tell me the old, old story.' Dolly sighed and arranged herself on a *chaise-longue*, lighting a cigarette, and tossing her chiffon scarf around her neck. 'I s'pose you've come to sponge some from me? I mighta guessed.'

'No, my angel, *mi amor*, it is just that your boss, he take us for a ride. He see us coming. He wring our necks like cheeken.' Chico dived on to the seat to shower her with kisses. 'It is just that you are more beautiful than the sunset. I do not want to come to you empty-handed.'

'Whoops! Watch it, you're spilling my drink. That's another stain on my dress.'

'*Sí*, that will not be the last one tonight. We will make hay, my leetle jumping frog.'

Dolly swung her legs to the ground, trying to finish her drink and hold him off. 'I ain't so sure I like the sunset allusion. Couldn't you say I'm like a fresh young dawn?' She gave a puff at the cigarette and stubbed it out. 'A jumping frog, eh? Well, that's a first, I must say.'

'What you do up here? This your office?'

'No, it's Patterson's. I take a break at eight an' cool off up here for an hour.'

'You and he – you are lovers?'

'Love don't really come into it, darlin'. But he's the boss man, ain't he? So, we do mingle socially, you might say, now and again.'

'That man, he is scoundrel. He—'

'Yeah, well, ain't we all?' Dolly grabbed the bottle, disentwined herself from Chico's octupus embrace, and advanced, somewhat unsteadily, to another door.'Follow me, Mr Mexico. He's got a nice feather bed in here. Maybe we oughta unwind.'

*

A half-hour later Lance Patterson burst into his office, followed by Reuben Horovitz and Buster Davis. 'So what you saying, Reuben?' He placed the two silver ingots on his desk. 'That he's got more of this stuff?'

'The way he's been giving it away, yes. First to two dumb prairie rats. Then to pay their debt. These samples are practically pure silver. If he's found a vein it will be worth a fortune.'

On the other side of the thin wooden wall Chico was lying naked in bed beside Dolly Darling, sweat trickling from brow and body from his recent exertions.

He was 'brought down from the clouds', as they say, by the sound of voices in the other room. He pressed an ear to the shiplap wall and could hear clearly. He put a finger to his lips to Dolly and whispered, 'I think we got company.'

'But where is the mine?' Lance hammered his fist on his desk. 'Ain't you got any idea, Reuben?'

'I've been searching those hills for five years; all those dry creeks and box canyons. If I knew where that silver vein was do you think I'd be standing here?'

'You musta got some idea,' Buster butted in. 'Didn't those two cowpokes say nuthin'?'

'No. They ain't as dumb as you think they are, in my opinion. But, before we go any further' –

Chico, in the other room, recognized the assayer's voice – 'I want one thing straight: we're in this together, you, me, and, I suppose, your employee here?'

'Together? Of course we are. If Crazy Ned's come across a pure seam we've hit the jackpot. We'll be partners, fifty-fifty. Buster, here, will be looked after.'

'OK?' – the assayer sounded hesitant – 'so I followed Crazy Ned, him and that girl, along to the restaurant. Got a table close to theirs. Listened in behind him.'

'So?' Lance demanded, impatiently. 'What did he say?'

'He's got a map he keeps in a canvas roll. He got it out his coat pocket and was showing it to her on the table. He mentioned some canyon, but I couldn't hear which, because of the damned clattering of the plates. That's all I know.'

'We need that map and I don't care how we get it. Where did they go?'

'They went over to Ned's wagon and headed back to his farm.'

'Come on. There's still an hour of daylight left 'fore sundown. Buster, get a couple of the boys and saddle up. We're going after them.'

Reuben sounded startled. 'You're not. . . ? I don't want to get involved in any killing.'

'We'll do what we have to do.' Lance gritted the words out, opened his desk drawer and pulled out a big Remington New Model Army revolver. Its solid frame over the cylinder made it the most reliable on the frontier. He loaded it with metal-jacket cartridges, stuffed it in his belt, and went to the bedroom to get his topcoat. He was surprised to see Dolly.

'What the hell you doing here?'

Dolly yawned and waved a gloved hand, airily. 'Oh, hello, you woke me. Having a nap, what's it look like? Suppose I've got to get up and go back down to that hellhole an' sing 'em some songs.'

Patterson stared at her lying with her knees up beneath the lumpy eiderdown. 'Sure, I don't pay you to sleep.'

He grabbed his coat and and hurried out. When she heard the door slam she drawled, 'You can come out now.'

Chico poked his dark-haired head up from between her knees and grinned. 'Do I have to? I like it down here.'

'All good things come to an end, sweetheart,' she said.

Back in his velveteens, sombrero and spurred boots, which Dolly had hurriedly hid under the bed at Lance's arrival, Chico stepped out on to the back stairs and watched Lance Patterson, Davis and two other men ride out of their stable and tear off out of town. 'Thees look bad,' he muttered. 'I better go get Tim.'

37

'What?' Tim Roberts cried, as Chico poked at him as he lay on a bed of straw in the livery quietly snoozing beside his horse. 'They've gone after Ned and his niece?'

'*Sí.* I fear there could be bad trouble.'

Tim jumped to his feet, buckled on his gunbelt, swung his saddle over the quarter horse. 'Come on, Brandy, gal. We got more work to do.'

Chico, too, had Satan saddled and bridled in double quick time. They sprang aboard, almost simultaneously, charged their mounts out of the livery and headed off hell for leather out of town.

The sun was sinking low as Ned Edwards drove his wagon along the winding trail through the rock-strewn Arizona landscape, the sky suddenly a bed of gold and blood red in the west. 'We're gonna be rich, Lucy. Rich beyond our wildest dreams. I allus told ya I'd find the pot at the end of the rainbow. Even you didn't believe me.'

'But, I've got a bad feeling about this, Uncle Ned. You don't need the money. You can come and live with us in Tombstone. You can retire in peace.'

'Peace? Ain't no peace in Tombstone, what with them Clantons and Earps feudin' and all them dregs of the frontier boozin' and whorin', if you'll excuse the phrase.'

'Oh, it's not so bad now Marshal Earp has cleared the Clantons out, although his poor brother, Virgil, did get crippled.'

'That's what I mean. It's no place for me, nor for a sweet gal like you. Look at these wide open spaces. God's own country. A man's got room to breathe. And a woman, too. Why don't you come and live out here? We could do up the ranch house now we're coming into cash, start a herd.'

'Well, it does have something.' Lucy hugged her knees, dreamily, as they rattled along. 'If a girl could find the right man, start a family. . . .'

'Heck, there's plenty men around. How about that youngster you met today? Tim. Weren't you taken by him? Even if he did lose the damn race.' He gave her a nudge with his elbow. 'Go on, admit it. I could tell he was taken by you.'

Lucy tried not to show she was startled. 'He's OK, but he's not husband material. He's just a down-at-heel drifter. He admitted it, himself.'

'Goldarn, it, gal. Cowboys git laid off in the winter months. There ain't nuthin' else to do but drift. True, the Mex is a tad crazy, but Tim's the right stuff. Him an' me, we're gonna get this mine operatin', you'll see—'

Just then there was the report of a revolver shot, and a bullet came whistling and whining above their heads. Ned looked around and saw the shadowy shapes of four men galloping along the trail after them.

'What in tarnation!' he cried. 'I don't like the look of this. Hang on, Lucy. We're being bushwhacked.' He reached for his rawhide whip and cracked it over the backs of the two wagon horses. 'Git outa here, ye mangy critters. Go on, move. Hee-agh!'

The two heavy horses sprang into a lumbering gait and then set off at a wild gallop along the ribbon of trail as more shots from behind startled them. The wagon bounced and rocked as they gathered speed and all Lucy could do was, indeed, hang on, and hope that a wheel didn't come off catapulting them into space. 'Who are they?' she cried.

'Hell knows. Some dang greedy varmints want my mine, I bet,' he shouted, whipping the horses some more. 'See that rifle under your feet. Git hold of it and start shootin'. Go on. Snap to it, gal.'

Lucy glanced back at the pursuing men who were about fifty yards behind and gaining on them. They appeared to be masked and obviously intent on doing evil. There was only one thing to do. She reached for the heavy Ballard. 'How does it work?' she yelled.

'Just jerk the lever. There's twelve shots in the magazine Go on, give 'em a taste of their own medicine.'

Lucy had done some shooting and was ready for the recoil as she turned and hugged the rifle into her shoulder. But it had a powerful kick and her first three shots went well wide. She gritted her teeth. How dare they? Who did they think they were? She took more careful aim, as best she could. The bullet ploughed into the chest of one of the horses, tumbling it and its rider to the ground. The poor horse struggled to rise, but succumbed into death. At least it had stopped them. They turned and milled about. But, as the wagon rounded a bend, she saw they had swung the fallen rider up behind one of them and were starting off again.

Lucy shuddered and gasped, 'They're not going to give up. They're coming on.'

'Is that so?' Ned yelled. 'Well, I'll show the varmints.' They were pulling up a rise amid the desolate, rocky landscape. He pulled the horses in, jumped down and took the Ballard from her hands. 'I'll stay here an' stop 'em. You drive on. Ranger Tom Archer's got a place five miles along the trail. You cain't miss the turning. Tell him to come quick.'

'But, what about you?' Lucy screamed. 'I can't leave you here.'

'Go on, do as you're told. Don't waste time. I'll be OK. I'm gettin' up behind that rock. Ride for your life, gal.' He slapped the horse's rump, setting them both off again. 'Hee-yagh!'

He watched Lucy, hanging on to the reins, go careering and bouncing along the trail again, looked back, saw the riders coming, levered a slug into the rifle, took a shot at them and ran for cover.

'It's me they're after, that's for sure,' Ned

muttered, as he rested the rifle barrel on a rock. 'She's safe now.' He peered into the gathering dusk. 'Come on, you cowardly rats. Come an' see if you can take a real man.' When no riders appeared on the trail, he said to himself, 'That's funny, where they gotten to?'

It was eerily silent, only the howl of a coyote in the distance. The hair prickled on the back of the old man's neck. He had a feeling they were creeping up on him, but from where?

'Hey, grandad!' Ned spun around and saw against the sunset the black silhouette of a man in a frock coat standing on a rock behind him. He swung the rifle to fire. But it was too late. There was a gunflash from the man's hand, an explosion, and a bullet blasted into Ned's chest, toppling him over . . . and slowly down into the dark sleep of eternity.

Lance Patterson jumped down and poked him with his boot-tip. 'Is he dead?' Davis asked, as he and the other two men joined him.

'Well, he ain't gonna be seeing the sunrise.' Lance knelt down and pressed Ned's eyelids closed. He didn't like the way he was staring at him. 'Now where's that map?'

He found the canvas roll in the dead man's coat pocket. 'This must be it,' he hissed out, spreading it, curiously. It was pencilled on the back of an old bill for purchase of corn. Difficult to interpret, various inverted v-marks to indicate hills, an arrowed trail pointing the way. . . .

Suddenly the four men heard the pounding of hoofs galloping along the trail from River Bend.

'Jesus!' Lance exclaimed. 'Who's that coming? Hastily he refolded the precious map into its container and stuffed it in the inside pocket of his suit, pushing the Remington back into his belt. 'Let's get back to the horses.'

Brandy's cream mane and tail were streaming out in the breeze as Tim sent her flying along the narrow dust trail, winding in and out of the terrain of weird wind-eroded boulders, up and down small hills. He had heard the sound of gunfire just behind the next rise. He rode up on to it and saw in the dusk four men running away from what appeared to be a body on the ground and clambering up among the rocks.

He whirled the quarter horse to a halt – she could spin on a silver dollar and stop at a gallop in thirty feet – jumped from the saddle and ran forward, drawing both Peacemakers, firing each at the fleeing bushwhackers. They reached the top of the pile of rocks and turned to return the leaden compliments. Lead fizzed past Tim's ears but he kept on firing, making them scurry for cover.

Chico arrived on the scene, vaulting from Satan's saddle to land beside his *compadre*. He, too, pulled out his Colt – an old cedar-gripped Navy converted to take metal cartridges – and let fly at the departing robbers.

'I don't like the look of this,' Tim yelled, running forward to glance down at Ned's body.

They both climbed up on to the rocks as fast as they could go, leaping from one smooth boulder to the other. But by the time they reached the pinnacle they saw that the murderers had ground-hitched their mounts down behind the outcrop and were heading away in a cloud of dust back towards River Bend.

'Shee-it!' Chico cried. 'We should have stayed on our horses and doubled back. We've lost them now.'

'Yeah.' Tim leapt back down from the boulders to the ground, his twin revolvers still gripped in his hands and stood over the corpse of Ned Edwards. 'Who'd'a thought they'd go this far? Poor old Ned.'

He spun around as they heard the sound of more drumming hoofs, but this time they were coming from the opposite direction. Two horses veered from the trail and charged towards them and Tim recognized Lucy, riding a piebald pony, accompanied by a fellow in fringed buckskins on a brindled stallion. He, too, had a revolver in his gloved hand, and leapt from the wild-eyed mustang to face them.

'OK, you two. Don't try anythang. Hand over your guns. I'm a lawman.'

Tom Archer was a man of slim, short stature, but like many so he made up for it with bantam-like bravado. He wore his fair hair hanging loose to his shoulders, frontier-style, beneath his hat, and he puffed out his check-shirted chest, his regard steely and unforgiving.

'Go on, do as I say. We've caught you red-handed.'

Lucy gave a scream of horror and jumped down on her knees over her uncle. 'Oh, my God! He's dead.'

'Yes, and these two rattlers killed him.'

'You're crazy,' Tim protested. 'We had nothing to do with this. Ned was our friend.'

'Some friends you were to him. I oughta plug you both. Look, your guns are still smoking. You flushed him out of his hiding place and killed him in cold blood.'

'Why should we do that?'

Lucy stared up at him, tears streaming from her eyes. 'For the map to the mine. You knew he had it on him, you filthy murderers. You wanted all that silver for yourselves. Oh, what a fool he was to trust you. And me too.'

'Lucy,' Tim pleaded. 'We didn't do this. We've just arrived on the scene and were firing at the men who—'

'Sure,' Tom Archer snapped. 'A likely story. Tell it to the judge. No use arguing, boys. Just hand over those pieces nice an' easy now.'

Chico backed away, his Colt at the ready. 'I ain't handing my gun to nobody. You ain't hanging me

45

for what we ain't done. You lousy greengo, you theenk I would do such a theeng. You insult my honour.'

'True, he insults mine, too. But it's no use having a shoot-out, Chico. That won't prove anything. That'll only make 'em more convinced that it was us. Come on, hand over your gun, *amigo*,' Tim said. 'We'll get out of this.'

He spun both of his nickel-plated Peacemakers, offering the staghorn butts to Archer. Reluctantly, Chico passed his Navy Colt across, too. 'I hope you know what you do, *amigo*. Already my neck, it begin to itch.'

'If we robbed Ned of his map,' Tim pointed out, 'then search us. Where is it? We ain't got it.'

'They probably had time to hide it in these rocks,' Archer told the girl, tucking the revolvers into his saddle-bags, then turning to take Lucy's elbow and raise her to her feet. 'You can't sit here grieving all night, gal. Git on the pony and go back to my place. The missus will see you're OK. I'll bring Ned's body in on the way back. I'm taking these two dingbats to jail.'

FOUR

'String 'em up,' an old woman cried as word spread around River Bend about what had happened and a mob congregated outside the jail. 'I knew them two racing cheats were up to no good.'

A burly farmer joined in the braying for instant rough justice. 'If you don't do it, Sheriff, we will.' His threat was echoed by a chorus of agreement. Old Ned had been a popular character.

Sheriff McBean was out of his element. A chubby fellow with a fat paunch, he liked the quiet life and had not been expecting trouble. 'You folks go home,' he shouted. 'These two'll be up before the judge in the mornin', *then* we'll hang 'em.'

He slammed the jail door shut and shoved the two prisoners into a barred cell, locking it with his ring of keys. The long-haired Archer stood arms akimbo, hands resting on his twin guns, and gave them his steely stare. He ran a small ranch but

47

worked when needed as a Ranger. He was renowned for bringing in his man, dead or alive. He had violently terminated the lives of many a malefactor, whether Mexican, Indian, black or white. He didn't believe in all that baloney about the process of law. His guns administered justice hereabouts.

'Maybe we should chuck 'em out to the mob,' he muttered. 'Say they broke out of jail?'

'Now, come on, Tom,' the sheriff hastily admonished. 'We can't do that. I'd have too much explaining to do.'

'Why are you so sure it was us?' Tim asked. 'Couldn't there be other suspects in this town?'

'You joking?' Archer quipped. 'Like who?'

'That assayer, for instance? He seemed mighty interested in where I got that silver nugget from. Why don't you two go question him?'

The sheriff raised a quizzical eyebrow to Archer. 'Maybe we oughta, Tom?'

'OK, let's go. I could do with a drink, anyhow.'

'Hey, another thing,' Tim called, as the two lawmen began to leave the jailhouse. 'There's one way of finding out where that bullet in Ned came from. Have the doc dig it out and examine it. If it's from a Colt it will have left-hand rifling.'

'What you talking about?' Archer turned to eye him. 'What's that prove?'

'If it's not from a Colt it will prove neither I nor Chico fired that shot.'

The sheriff scratched his jaw. 'Howja mean?'

Tim sighed with exasperation. 'Surely you know it's a fact that all Colt bullets spiral to the left as they leave the barrel, both handguns and rifles.

Archer gave a scoffing smirk. 'You don't, say?'

'Yes, I do say. It's the traditional way Colts have always been made. But all other handguns' bullets rifle to the right. That, come to think of it, includes Remingtons' – he suddenly remembered the big revolver Lance Patterson had used to start the race meet – 'and there's a few of those around this town.'

'Come on, Sheriff,' Archer said. 'I ain't never heard such a load of bull. We'll leave these bozos to stew in their own juice. You ain't got long to be in the land of the living, boys. You'd better be ready to repent your sins by the time we get back.'

The door of the jail was slammed and locked. Tim Roberts sank down on a bunk with a grimace. 'Them lunkheads have got us kicking air already. A nice mess we're in.'

'*Sí*, and this jail is solid adobe. We Mexicans knew how to build. We won't dig our way out of here tonight.'

In his office above the Silver Cartwheel, Lance Patterson sat at his desk and pored over the all but illegible map. 'What'n hell does this mean?'

Reuben and Buster Davis leaned over his shoulders and offered suggestions. 'That big shape must

49

be Miller Peak. So the mine is due south-west of there,' Reuben said.

'Yeah, but it could be anywhere.' Buster prodded his thick finger at the map. 'That scrawl don't make much sense to me.'

Lance stroked his clean-shaven jaw. 'There's one person who should know. That niece of Ned's. You say he was talking to her all about it in the restaurant? She'll know the exact spot.'

'Shall I go get her, boss?' Davis asked. 'If I break a couple of her fingers she'll soon squeal.'

'She's at the Archer place tonight, but she'll probably go back to Ned's place tomorrow. We'll get her then. I'm afraid she'll have to be eliminated, too.'

'Is that necessary?' Reuben protested, a worried frown on his face.

'It certainly is, unless you want it to be us three up on that scaffold they're busy building instead of them two cowboy hicks. Maybe you should pull the trigger this time, Reuben, so we're all part of this?'

'No.' Sweat broke out on the assayer's brow. 'I couldn't do that. She's a mere girl—'

'Who's a mere girl?' Darling Dolly asked, as she burst into the office without knocking. 'What are you three up to?'

'Why don't you mind your own business, you stupid hoo-er,' Lance snapped, quickly opening a drawer to hide the canvas-covered map. 'Or it might be you whose services we're dispensing with.

I was just saying we've got to cut down on girl-power in this establishment. We'll have to sack a couple.'

'Oh, yeah? You seem to be doing pretty well out of us as far as I can see. You chisel us out of most of our fair share of earnings, anyway.'

'Don't come busting in here without knocking telling me how to run my business.' Lance got to his feet with a certain menace to his regard. 'Who do you think you are? You're not indispensable, yourself, Dolly. You're getting a bit long in the tooth.'

If a look could kill, Dolly's would have shattered him on the spot. 'So, you figure you don't owe me nuthin', Lance, for the years I've put in helping to build up this dump?'

'He don't owe you a thing, darlin',' Davis growled. 'Doncha forget that.'

'What do you want, anyway?' Lance asked, testily.

'It's my boyfriend. He's in the lock-up. I need to borrow some cash to bail him out.'

'Your boyfriend? You mean that crazy Mex?' All three men laughed roughly, at her flustered look. 'So you've fallen for a greaser kid half your age, is that it? Nobody's gonna bail him out, nor his pal, Roberts. They're both gonna swing.'

'You know Chico had nothing to do with killing Ned. He hasn't got a malicious bone in his body. Neither has Tim for that matter.'

51

'Men do strange things, missy,' Reuben said, with an oily smile, 'when it comes to silver and gold.'

'Yes, they do, don't they?' Dolly gave them a curious look. 'Are you sure you didn't have nuthin' to do with this, Lance?'

'Me? You gone crazy, too, Dolly? Me, Buster, Reuben here, too, were in this office all night. We never left the saloon.' He suddenly caught Dolly by her scarf, pulled her to him. 'You remember, surely? Or were you too drunk? But that's what you're going to testify to if the sheriff should ask.'

Dolly returned his stare with her pale-blue eyes defiantly. 'And if I don't?'

'If an old hoo-er like you got pulled out of the river,' Davis said, 'they would conclude that she'd had enough and took her own life.'

Lance thrust her tottering away towards the door. 'Remember that, Dolly, darling.'

When she had gone he grinned at the others. 'Things couldn't have worked out better. Soon as those two take the drop we'll get rid of the girl and move in on the mine. Boys, I think it's time to celebrate.'

Dolly twisted and turned all night in her bunk in a wooden cubicle allotted her on the top floor of the saloon, similar to the other girls' – you could hardly call it a room. For what remained of the night, that is, she got very little sleep. Sure, the years kept turning; she was getting on. Was that her fault? But she still had that certain something that lit a fellow's candle, she knew that. She had always had it, even as a 14-year-old girl. Maybe that was what had led her astray in the first place, being the flame around which men fluttered like foolish moths. But it was she who had become the fool, trusting a man like Lance Patterson. Sure, she knew he was a chiseller. But she had never thought he might be a murderer. And a fool for falling for this new boy, Chico. She knew what he was, a Latino love 'em and leave 'em type. A wanderer, a lovable rogue, a carefree stud who had no intention of being roped by some woman twenty years older than him. Woman? A whore they had called her. Their jeering laughter still rang in her ears. It was true, plenty of whores ended up in the river. All played out, unable to face the emptiness ahead, of being old, unwanted, with nowhere to go.

'I'm not a whore,' she hissed out. 'I'm an exotic dancer, a singer, an entertainer.' She swung out of bed and lit the candle, unable to sleep. 'What shall I do?'

A voice in her head replied, 'Dolly, if you've got any sense, keep out of it.'

'Why should I?' she asked it. 'What have I got to lose?'

Now I'm talking to myself, she thought. I must be going crazy. She lit a cigarette from the candle and prepared to wash and put on the same old stained red dress. Time she bought another one. Dawn's light was beginning to seep through the curtain. The French girl in the next cubicle was snoring lustily. She was young; she had no worries. Outside, the barkeep, Ned, was unpadlocking the grille across the batwing doors, opening up for any early customers, preparing for another day.

How the hell was she going to get those boys out of jail? They were up before the judge today and a carpenter had already been busy building a scaffold in the main square for their hanging. Folks liked a good double-hanging. They would get quite a send-off.

Lance Patterson had woken early, too. He usually went across to the barber shop for the hot towel treatment. But today he carefully shaved himself with a cut-throat. He splashed away the suds and stroked his velvety jaw. Yes, he was certainly a good-looking guy in the prime of life. He squeezed his dimpled chin and smiled at himself. His plan to get rich quick was going well. There would be thousands of dollars of ore in that mine and he intended to have it. What good would it have been to that silly old fool, Ned? He would have died soon, anyway. Once those two busybody cowpokes were strung up there was no reason why anybody should suspect him. Once they'd got the information they needed from the girl he would get Davis to dispose of her, break her neck, make it look like a fall from the wagon. There would be that greedy old fool Reuben to unload, too. No way he was splitting with him. Maybe, later, he would backshoot Davis down some dark alley. And Dolly? Yes, he would have to let her go. There must be no come-back. He would be rich and there would be nobody to put the screws on him.

Lance smiled at his image in the glass once more as he brushed back his brilliantined hair. 'It'll be easy,' he said, with a shrug. 'Dead men tell no tales. Nor women, neither.'

He put on his jacket and went down to the bar. Darling Dolly was already there, perched on her usual stool, her face the colour of flour, her eyes outlined in black, her lips and cheeks rouged. 'You're up early,' he said.

'Yeah, I needed a stiffener,' she replied, fiddling with her drink before tossing it back. 'Gimme another, Ned.'

First the 'keep placed an Irish coffee before Lance, his usual breakfast, fifty per cent coffee, fifty whiskey. The boss stirred it and muttered, 'I hope you've taken our little chat last night to heart. You can stay on here but I want to know whose side you're on.'

'I know where my bread's buttered. You more or less own me, don't you, Lance? Where else could I go?'

'Well, just remember that.' When his bodyguard, Davis, came downstairs, he beckoned him over. 'Get the horses ready to go. Bring four of the boys.'

'What about Reuben?'

'No, he's no damn use. He's too weak-kneed.'

He watched Davis go, gave a few curt orders to the 'keep and a cleaning woman, finished his coffee and nodded to Dolly. 'Look after the shop. We'll be back for the trial this afternoon. Don't let 'em start the hanging without me.'

Dolly gave him a weak smile and drawled, 'Sure.'

When he had gone, cantering his horse out of town with Davis and his men by his side, Dolly tossed her purple chiffon scarf around her throat and said she was taking a stroll for some fresh air.

Outside, the town was slowly coming back to life, storekeepers opening up, sweeping the dust out on to the sidewalks, arranging their produce in baskets. Dolly walked along to a clapboard cabin, a notice on its front in crude red paint proclaiming, 'Mining Supplies.'

'You're my first customer,' the owner called out. 'How can I help you, lady?'

'I need some dynamite. A coupla sticks with fuse wires and so forth.'

'Why, 'he scoffed, 'you going mining?'

'Nope. If it's any of your business I got a friend. She's got a well. It's blocked. Thought if we tossed a couple of sticks down it might open it up.'

'Might do the trick,' the man said, serving her. 'But be careful of this stuff. Don't blow yourselves up.'

'Try not to.' Dolly paid him and put the dynamite in her bag. 'No need to wrap it. Many thanks. Good morning.'

'Have a good morning yourself, ma'am.'

'I'll try to,' Dolly trilled, as she stepped out and strolled back past the scaffold to the jailhouse. The door in the abobe wall was locked. The sheriff would still be fast asleep in the boarding-house down the street. Dolly went round the back, looked in the stable. The quarter horse and the black mustang were there. They eyed her, inquisitively. 'Time to saddle up, boys. Or are you a girl?'

Dolly saddled and bridled them as best she could, although she wasn't quite sure if she'd got the mustang's latigo strap and the mare's martingale right. 'That oughta do.'

There was a barred window in the adobe, high on the wall. She found a box, stood it on end, and climbed up to peer through. Tim and Chico were stretched out on their bunks.

'When's that lousy fat pig of a sheriff gonna come and bring us some coffee?' Chico was asking. 'I sure am tired of listening to that hammering out in the square.'

'Yeah, I expect they'll be starting again soon,' Tim replied. 'Sheriff says they're building an eight-foot-high platform, two trapdoors and scaffolds, with plenty of room to drop. They are certainly going to an awful lot of trouble on our behalf.'

'Psst!' a voice hissed. 'Perhaps you might disappoint those folks.' Then it sang out, 'Better is to live and die under a pirate flag, say I.'

'What?' Chico jumped from his bunk. 'Who was that?'

'It's Darling Dolly.' Tim saw her peeping through the bars. 'Maybe she's brought us some coffee.'

'I've brought you better than that.' She giggled as she teetered on the wooden box. 'Your ticket out.'

'*Caramba*! *Mi amor*, how wonderful to see you. But what you talk about?'Chico jumped up to try to kiss her through the bars. 'Is it really you? Am I dreaming?'

'You'll find out. If I were you two I'd squat down in that corner and pull those palliasses over you.'

'Why?'

'I've got some dynamite. I'm gonna blow a hole in this wall. You ready? I'll light the fuse.'

'Oh, no!' Chico cried, as he and Tim scrambled to pull their palliasses from the bunks. 'I knew Dolly was wild. But I did not know she crazy. Quick, take cover, *amigo*.'

They cowered in the corner as the seconds slowly ticked by. 'What's she playing at?' Tim asked.

Suddenly, it was like all hell was let loose. There was a flash and crash and a blast as the wall caved in and showered the cell with debris. The shock wave even demolished the sheriff's desk.

'My ears!' Chico poked his sombrero'd head

through a heap of adobe bricks and dust. 'She has deafened me.'

Tim climbed out from behind his mattress. 'She certainly doesn't waste time. Look, the cell door's been blown right off its hinges.'

As the dust and powdersmoke drifted, Dolly poked her head through the hole. 'Howdy, boys.I got your horses waiting.

Tim hurriedly collected their guns from the hooks above the sheriff's now broken desk and tossed Chico his. 'Come on,' he said. 'We must have woken up the whole town.'

'My leetle cactus flower, you have saved my life.' Chico leaped out of the hole and embraced Darling Dolly. He hugged and kissed her. 'I am your humming bird. I would love to suck the nectar from all your flowers.'

'Put her down,' Tim snapped. 'You can do your humming some other time. Right now I want you to cause a diversion out front.'

'*Sí*, that easy.' Chico leapt on to Satan and grinned as he hauled him around with one hand and brandished his old Navy Colt in the other. 'What *you* do?'

'I want to try to find that map before I go.'

'Patterson's office is empty,' Dolly cried. 'He's gone out of town. Now's your chance.'

'You got any more of that dynamite?'

'Yes, I only used one stick.'

'Good.' He left Brandy in the stable, took Dolly's

hand and went at a run along the back of the houses towards the saloon. 'You wait here,' he said, when they reached the wooden back stairs.

'No, I've got a key to the door.' She led the way up and unlocked. Cautiously, she poked her head inside. 'Come on.'

There was the blamming of revolvers from the main street. 'Chico's doing his stuff.'

'I saw Lance put that canvas-covered map in his desk drawer.' Dolly took a look. 'No, it's gone.'

'It's probably in the safe, if he hasn't got it with him.' Tim held out his hand. 'Give me that dynamite. We'll blow it apart.'

He put the stick under the safe door, paid out the fuse, lit it, then took cover with Dolly in a corner behind the up-turned *chaise-longue*.

Karoom! Glass, ornaments, shattered furniture flew everywhere. Tim took a look through the roiling dust. The safe door was hanging from its hinges. He looked inside among the tin boxes of cash. 'Here it is,' he cried, jubilantly. 'This proves he killed Ned.'

'Yes,' Dolly said, 'but who's going to believe us?'

There was a hammering on the door, men's voices out on the landing of the saloon. 'Quick,' Tim yelled, grabbing her hand again. 'Time to get out of here.'

Out on the main street Chico was charging Satan back and forth having a fine old time hurrahing the town, shooting over the heads of storekeeps, making them dive for cover, sending bullets whistling to smash windows and lamps. But, suddenly he felt his saddle cinch slipping. Dolly had failed to tighten it enough. Slowly, inexorably, he began to slip to one side until he was hanging almost under the horse's belly. 'Holy Moses!' he cried, as he lost his stirrups and tumbled to the ground, narrowly avoiding Satan's iron-shod hoofs. He sat in the dust, his head spinning, wondering what had happened to his gun.

At the back of the saloon Tim was halfway down the wooden steps when three of Patterson's boys came running round to look for him. The lithe young cowboy let them start up towards him then leapt boots first at them. He knocked them flying like skittles, gave a mighty right to the jaw to one who tried to grab hold of him, sending him sprawling, skipped over the clutches of the other two, and ran for the stable along at the jail.

Dolly watched him escape, smiled to herself, and discreetly withdrew back into the wrecked office. She was about to unlock the door to the saloon when she remembered the piles of cash in the safe. 'Why not?' she said, helping herself to a bundle and stuffing it in her bag. 'He owes me.'

'What's all the commotion?' she asked, innocently, as she went downstairs to the bar.

Tim Roberts came charging out from the back of the jail on Brandy, the mare's muscles rippling beneath her coat, her neck arched proudly, restrained by the martingale for otherwise she was a stargazer, her cream mane and tail tossing as she trotted down the street.

When he saw Chico kneeling on the ground looking for his Colt unaware that a butcher in a striped apron had come to the door of the meat market with a hog-killer gun in his hands he shouted a warning, 'Watch out!'

Chico screamed with fear as he looked up into the barrels of the hog-killer and, as it exploded with a mighty roar, leapt for safety. 'He try to keel me!' he cried amid a volley of Spanish oaths. He spotted his Colt by a water butt and crawled to retrieve it.

'Jump up!' Tim shouted and hauled him up behind him. The townspeople had begun to join in the battle seeing their hang-ees trying to escape. One man fired a revolver from his bedroom window. Another aimed a shotgun from his shop doorway. But both Tim and Chico on board Brandy were blazing away with their six-guns making them jump back for safety.

Satan, his saddle dangling beneath him, had struggled along for fifty yards and stood looking bemused. Chico jumped down and caught him, hefting the saddle straight, and jerking the cinch and latigo tight as Tim covered him. Then amid a volley of whistling lead from all sides they set off at a sprint along the main drag.

The obese Sheriff McBean had run from his

boarding-house, an upraised rifle in his hands. Tim charged Brandy into him and McBean jumped for his life. He recovered in time to send a shot whistling to no avail after the absconders as they sprinted round a corner and headed out of town.

FIVE

Crazy Ned's tumbledown shack was deserted when Lance Patterson, Buster Davis and four rough-looking *hombres* cantered in on their horses. No smoke from the chimney, the corral empty. It was still early morning. 'Maybe she's still over at the Archer place?' Lance hazarded. 'Maybe she's decided to stay there 'til the funeral. If so, we got a problem.'

'So, what we gonna do?'

'We'll hide the horses among those willows and kick our heels for a while.'

However, they had barely been waiting ten minutes when they saw Lucy driving in the wagon, the straight-backed Ranger Tom Archer, with his long flowing hair, riding alongside.

'They're getting something out of the wagon,' Davis muttered. 'Looks like Ned's corpse. They're carrying him into the house.'

'Guess she's planning on planting him out back someplace. We better make our move before the coffin-maker and preacher arrive.'

They waited impatiently for Archer to leave, but it wasn't long before he came out, jumped on his mount and with a wave to the girl rode away.

'Now we'll get her,' Lance said, as she went back into the house. 'You guys wait here. Come on, Buster.' He and Davis hitched their horses outside and didn't bother to knock, barging in on her.

'What do you want?' she cried.

'That's simple. You're gonna show us the way to that old fool's mine.' Lance gave a grimace of cynical distaste as he glanced at her dead uncle stretched out on the kitchen table. 'Phew! He's startin' to stink up the place. Time he was six feet under.'

'How dare you come pushing in here? Who do you think you are? You had better get out before—'

'Before?' Davis grabbed the girl's slim arms and twisted them behind her. 'Before what?'

'Who do I think I *am*?' Lance echoed her. He put a hand in her hair and gave her two vicious slaps across the face. 'I'm in charge from now on. You better remember that.'

Lucy recoiled, her cheek reddening from the blows. She blinked back tears and met his eyes, defiantly. 'How do I know where the mine is? He never told me.'

'We heard different. You were overheard in that restaurant in town. He was telling you how to get there.'

'Don't be absurd.' Lucy gasped with pain as Davis twisted her arms some more. 'Tell him to stop. That hurts.'

Lance gave a bitter laugh, twisted his fingers in her hair and gave it a jerk. 'We haven't even started yet.'

'Shall I break her arms, boss?'

'Not yet. That's up to her. She's got to use them to ride if she's going to show us the way. Come on, sweetheart, be sensible.' Lance smiled in his conceited way at her, stroking Lucy's cheek with his spare hand. 'Say, you're a pretty li'l thang, aincha?' Suddenly he caught hold of her blouse and tore it apart, then ripped open her cotton chemise exposing her pale, pink-tipped breasts. 'Just look at them titties. Whooee! Maybe we could do this a different way? Howja like to be thrown to my dogs, girlie?' He dropped his hand, pulling up her skirt over her knees, trying to grope a hand between her legs. 'We got four more men outside who'd love to give it you.'

'Don't!' Lucy shrilled, wriggling and kicking out at him with a booted foot. 'You filthy bastard. Leave me alone. They will hang you for this.'

Lance grinned at her. 'Let's take her into the bedroom, Buster, an' have some fun. I'll go first, then it'll be your turn. Then we'll toss her to the men.'

'I dunno about that, Lance.' The surly sidekick was not averse to inflicting pain, but most men in the West, even out-and-out villains, had an ingrained respect for a virtuous woman. 'I can't do that. It wouldn't be right. She's a decent gal.'

'Oh, so you've turned into a gentleman all of a sudden? Well, I'll tell you one thing: there's no such thing as a decent gal. They're all the same.' He pinched and squeezed Lucy's nipples, tightening his grip in her hair. 'See her squirm.'

'You're hurting me,' Lucy cried.

'Yeah, you'll be squirming once I start on you. You'll love it. Maybe I'll break you in an' sell you to a brothel over the border? They'd pay a good price for a *decent* white gal with your looks. How about *that*, sister?'

'For Christ's sake, just tell us where the mine is,' Davis growled, 'before I break your fingers one by one.'

'She thinks I don't mean what I say.' Lance put his face close to hers as if to lick her lasciviously with his tongue.

Lucy spat in his face. 'You're going to regret this,' she shouted. 'I have friends. They will track you down.'

Lance recoiled, wiped the spittle from his face, and slapped her again, but angrily and harder. 'Who are your friends, huh? Those two dumb creeps who are gonna take the fall for shootin' Crazy Ned?'

'Come on,' Davis urged, 'all you got to do is show us the way to the mine. That stoopid map we took from Ned didn't make no sense at all.'

'So it was you who killed him?' Lucy's violet eyes blazed with anger as she stared at Lance. 'I should have known. There was me accusing Tim. What a fool I've been.'

'Yeah, funny, ain't it?' Lance quipped. 'What a pity you won't be able to be at his hanging.'

'You . . . oh, what do I care about the silly mine. What do I want it for? It didn't do my uncle any good and I doubt if it will you. Just leave me alone. I'll show you the way, if you promise to let me go when I do.'

'Sure,' Lance soothed, releasing his hand from her hair. 'Of course we'll let you go, if you promise not to say anything about this. Is that a deal?'

'Yes, it's a deal. You're welcome to the rotten mine. Uncle Ned's instructions weren't very clear but I'll do my best to find it.'

'That's the spirit,' Davis growled, patting her back. 'You go put on a decent blouse, your hat'n coat an' we'll be on our way. I'll go saddle your bronc. Don't worry now, Lance didn't mean those things he said about taking you to Mexico.'

Lance raised a quizzical eyebrow as she went into the other room. 'Didn't I?'

Patterson, Davis, the four desperadoes, and the girl had barely been gone half an hour, heading up into the maze of boulder-strewn hills, when Tim and Chico galloped their sweat-streaming horses into the small ranch only to find the shack deserted, but for a corpse.

'There ain't nobody else home,' Tim Roberts said. 'I wonder where Lucy could be? If she brought Ned's body back she must have been here.'

'Old Crazy Ned, he certainly was not house-proud.' Chico surveyed the clutter in the kitchen, dirty pots and pans, kindling scattered about the stove, smelly socks and old clothes, unwashed tin plates and remains of food festering in a bowl; there was rancid bacon grease on the table with the stub of a candle in a pile of melted wax. The back room was not much better, a pile of filthy blankets on the bed. 'Whoo! Didn't he ever open a window?'

Tim was stroking his chin, eyeing the white-bearded old prospector's body sprawled on what would have been in other households a dining-table. There was a dried patch of blood around a hole torn in his plaid shirt on his chest where the bullet must have ploughed in. He heaved him up, stiff with rigor mortis, and examined his back. It had not come out the other side. 'It must be still in there.' Tim pulled a razor-sharp knife from a sheath on his belt. 'I'm gonna take a look.'

He cut the shirt and filthy woollen undervest away and made a neat incision around the hole. 'Looks like it's blasted right into the heart. See?"

'No.' Chico made a queasy face. 'I rather not.'

Tim poked around, his nostrils twitching at the stench. 'Got it,' he said, fishing out the large bullet with his fingers and holding it aloft.

'Hold it right there, you polecats!' Tom Archer kicked open the door and strode inside, his twin revolvers in his fists aimed at them. 'Or I'll blast ye to hell.'

'Fair cop!' Chico exclaimed, raising his hands with alacrity. 'Don't shoot, meester. I geeve in.'

'You better, buddy.' The cocky little lawman in his fringed leathers eyed them sternly from beneath the brim of his hat. 'How about you, son? You better keep your hands cool 'less you wanna be trading hot lead.'

'Look what I've found in him, Ranger. 'Tim wiped the bullet clean of blood on Ned's shirt. 'You see the rifling on that? The regular kind, goes to the right. Any gun expert will tell you that was never fired from a Colt and that's the only kind of gun Chico and I carry. I'd lay an even bet this came from Lance Patterson's Remington.'

'Don't give me all that bull again.' But his grey eyes flickered with interest as he looked at the bullet. 'Where's Lucy, that's what I want to know?'

'How should we know?' Chico said. 'She not here.'

'I thought they said she was staying at your place.'

'She was, but I dropped her off here this morning. I was going back when I saw your dust and drew off the trail. Nearly shot you down as you passed. You were going at quite a lick.'

'*Sí*, a man does ride fast if he break out of jail.'

'We broke out to prove our innocence and this says it wasn't us.' Tim brandished the bullet, then took Dan's canvas-covered map from his coat pocket. 'We found this in Patterson's safe. Darling Dolly, as they call her, will testify to that.'

Ranger Archer slowly lowered his shiny, nickel-plated revolvers and replaced them in his holsters. 'Looks like I may have misjudged you boys. But where's Lucy, that's what I asked?'

'Dolly said they left town early this morning, Lance Patterson and those bully-boys of his, and headed this way.' Tim suddenly spotted among all the grime a clean piece of torn material. He picked it up from the floor. 'I could swear that this is from the blouse she was wearing. I don't like the look of this at all. If they have manhandled that girl I'll kill them.'

Archer strutted into the back room and emerged holding the torn blouse aloft. 'Here's the rest of it. Looks like they let her change before they left. Come on, boys, we're wasting time.'

He went out at a run, caught his horse and vaulted into the saddle, swinging the grey around. 'Make sure your water bottles are filled, boys, and your guns are loaded. That's all you're gonna need.'

They set off towards the hills, Tim frowning at

71

the map in his hand. 'This ain't gonna be a lot of good but it's all we've got.'

'The ground iss hard as iron,' Chico remarked. 'It not going to be easy to follow trail.'

'We've got to try,' Tim said. 'Once they get to the mine I hate to think what they'll do to Lucy.'

Reuben Horovitz jammed his black derby hat down hard around his ears to stop it from falling off every time he bent over to pick up a rock. Rock? You could call it that: the most valuable rocks he had come across in a long time, veined with pure silver. He staggered out of the entrance hole to Crazy Ned's mine with another clutched in his arms and threw it on to the pile in his wagon.

'I certainly fooled Lance Patterson.' He spoke to the pair of wagon horses for lack of any other audience. 'Pretended I couldn't hear what Ned said to that gal about Latigo Canyon, about how to find the mine, pretended I couldn't make head or tail of that map. I know these hills as good as any lone coyote. He thinks he's so smart and high and mighty. *Trust* him to go fifty-fifty! Huh! I'd sooner trust a rattlesnake.'

Reuben had headed out from River Bend well before dawn with the wagon and had found the deserted mine before sun-up. He had been mightily surprised to find what he did inside the front cavern, a pile of ore already hacked from the walls of the mine and hauled out all ready for transportation.

'All we got to do now is get it to Bisbee.' Sweat was trickling from his brow as the sun climbed high. 'We'll take the back trails so we don't run into nobody. Another couple of rocks and that'll be about as much as you two critters can manage. No need to be greedy.'

When he had piled on three more lumps of ore he hung on to the wagon breathing hard. When he got to Bisbee he would register the mine in his own name and hire a bunch of gallows-bird shootists of his own. 'Let Patterson try and run me off then,' he muttered.

He tried to brush the dust from his pin-striped suit and couldn't resist sticking a small magnifying glass in his eye to study one of the rocks again. Yes, he could hardly believe it. There must be $500 worth in just one of those rocks. 'I'll cash these in, come back and set up a proper mining organiztion. I won't sell out to nobody.'

Time to get moving. He glanced up at the sun, put the glass back in his pocket, gathered the reins and stuck one boot up to haul himself on to the box. He froze as a mocking cackle of laughter drifted to him. . . .

Reuben stood with one foot up on the wheel and slowly looked around to see Lance Patterson sitting his horse on a rise above him, gradually joined by five other men, who clambered their mounts up to form a semi-circle around him. The assayer swallowed spittle, unable to speak as fear turned the sweat cold on his back.

'Well, whadda ya know?' Lance gave another mocking giggle. 'Just look at this. Our pard Reuben thought he could help himself 'fore we got here. I shoulda known not to trust him.'

Reuben was not a man who wore a gunbelt. He turned to them and raised his open hands, shrugging, trying to smile. 'What you talkin' about, Lance? I been waiting for you to arrive. I been making a start on getting some ore out.'

Lance smiled, widely. 'So I see.'

Reuben nodded his head. 'Would I try to cheat you?'

'That's the question. Would you?' Lance fingered the Remington stuck in his belt. 'Waal, you snivellin' li'l rat, yes, it looks like you sure might try.'

'No need to be rude, Lance,' Reuben said. 'Them ain't nice words.'

'They sure ain't, but they suit you, you creep, don't they?' Lance rode his mustang down the slope and called out, 'Bring the girl.'

When Lucy on her horse was led forward by one of the men, Reuben gaped at her. 'What you *doing*? You're not going to kill her, are you?'

'She'll get what's coming to her,' Lance spat out. 'Same as you will, Reuben.' He looked around him. 'So this is the famous mine, an' you knew its whereabouts all the time. He's been holding out on us, boys.'

'No,' Reuben protested. 'You have got this all wrong. I just had a hunch I might know where it was so I came out to take a look. I was going to bring these samples back to show you. Actually, this ore, it's not so hot. Maybe we're wasting our time.'

'Maybe *you* are.' Lance still had his fingers playing on the butt of his Remington. He didn't want to fire a shot, just in case somebody had followed them and was in the vicinity. 'What shall we do with him, boys?'

'Break his damn neck,' Davis growled, 'and toss him off the cliff.'

The other four men laughed in an ugly way at his words. They were just dregs of the frontier, hard-eyed men, down on their luck, whom Patterson had hired. The only qualification necessary was that they could shoot a gun and use it to kill without question, if necessary.

The oldest one, Raker, hunched up in a tall hat and a long, tarp rain-cheater, spat out a gob of baccy at Reuben. 'I'd be glad to take care of him for you, Lance.'

'Maybe we oughta teach him a lesson first.' The youngest, Rafe Thompson, grinned a mouthful of bad teeth. 'How about we tie him across that wheel an' I'll put my snake across him.' He lovingly stroked a rawhide whip coiled in his hands. 'I'll cut him to the bone for you.'

Reuben's grey-tinged spade beard waggled as he protested. 'Don't be foolish, boys. You got to believe me, I'm here to help you. I'm a good friend of yours, Lance. You need me: I know about mining.'

Patterson nodded to a paunchy, dim-witted rustler, named Randall, who was holding the girl's horse. 'Take her into the mine. Tie her up. Tight! Make sure she don't escape. I got plans for her.'

'This is a bad mistake you're making, Lance,' Reuben gabbled on. 'No need for killing. We can run this mine legally. I don't want trouble, Lance.'

Lance turned to the fourth man. 'Rusty, you take this two-timing louse up along the cliff. There's a five hundred foot drop along-a-ways. Don't shoot him. Just tell him *adios*. You understand?'

'Sure.' The scrawny, red-haired bully boy, in range clothes, gave a flicker of a smile, and moved his bronc towards Reuben. 'Move it, creep. You're coming with me.'

'That may not be so.' Suddenly Reuben brought from his jacket pocket a two-shot derringer, a stubby little pearl-handled piece. He aimed point blank at Rusty, who howled as the .22 cut through his forearm making him drop his own revolver like it was a hot brick. 'One for you, Lance?'

Patterson's face registered astonishment that the assayer could pull such a trick, then he ducked and swung his mount around to avoid the discharge.

Reuben didn't waste a moment of time. He hauled himself on to the wagon box, grabbed the reins and gave a wild scream to the pair to get moving. 'Hee-yagh!'

They didn't need much urging, startled out of their torpor already by the gunshots. They reared up and away down the incline as Raker loosed his six-gun after Reuben. Young Rafe, too, dropped his whip and reached for his rifle.

'Hold it, boys,' Lance shouted. 'You stay here. This is going to be my pleasure. I'll wring the neck of that li'l rat.'

He put spurs to his mustang and went racing away after the wagon down the dusty trail. Reuben had maybe given his horses too much encouragement and was fighting to control them as the over-loaded wagon thrust them forward and was veering dangerously close to a steep precipice that ran alongside the trail. The assayer gritted his teeth and tried to apply the brake as bullets whistled past his head, The wagon began to sway from side to side. 'Whoa down,' he yelled in panic. 'Steady now.' But, basically, he, like the horses, had one aim in mind – to get away.

SIX

'There's another!' Ranger Tom Archer scanned the hard ground and pointed to a purple bean in a crevice of rock. 'There ain't many of 'em but they're sure pointing the way.'

Before leaving the shack Lucy had snatched up a small bag of kidney beans from the kitchen table and hid them in her pocket. As she rode, dragged along on a leading rein by one of Patterson's men, she had discreetly dropped them here and there. She wasn't sure how far they had to go so she couldn't be too generous.

As they followed, Tim Roberts had been picking out the easier recognizable points on the map. They had climbed slowly, higher and higher, to about 1,000 feet around the side of Miller Peak. 'There's the saddleback between two hills,' he announced, aiming towards it. 'Then it looks like we gotta go up through a forest of soo-ar-roh, if that's what these little signs on the map mean.'

'Crazy Ned,' Chico sighed, as he leapt his horse upwards,' he not a good map arteest.'

Archer kept an eye out for the trail of beans, difficult to follow, but gradually, yes, leading them up through the forest of saguaro, the strange cacti with upraised arms as if beseeching rain, that grew on one of the slopes. They had made their way on through the jumble of rocks and come across a fork in a narrow trail that led up higher around the edge of a deep cut canyon.

Suddenly they heard gunshots, the echoes bouncing off the walls of the canyons. 'That's up ahead,' the Ranger shouted. 'Come on, let's move it.'

But as Tim urged his powerful quarter horse on up the rocky trail he saw a wagon, dragged by two wildly prancing horses, careering down the curving trail towards them. It was about a quarter of a mile away but he could distinguish what appeared to be two men struggling on top of the wagon. 'They're gonna go over if they don't watch out,' he cried.

Lance Patterson and Reuben Horovitz were indeed fighting to the death on the back of the wagon. It had been difficult for Lance to catch up and manoeuvre alongside the bouncing truck, but he had leapt from his horse and landed on the silver ore. He had jumped forward and put a stranglehold around the throat of the assayer, pulling him backwards from the box. He had imagined it would be easy to land a knock-out punch to Reuben's jaw, but the older man was made of sterner stuff, kicking, biting, fighting like a weasel, as he toppled back on top of him, trying to gouge out Lance's eyes with his thumbs. . . .

They had struggled to their feet and were raining blows on each other, tripping and cursing, stumbling on the rocks as the wagon rocked from side to side. The two men fought on like wild animals, swinging fists at each other, seemingly unaware of their imminent fate.

A wagon wheel hit a rock and went flying through the air, the body of the buckboard began to creak and disintegrate, and suddenly the horses broke free from their harness as, for seconds, Lance and Reuben stood poised, as in a frieze, staring at a vast vista of space looming up. . . .

Then they were over the rimrock as the wagon tipped over the cliff and went bouncing and crashing down the precipice for a thousand feet. Finally it came to a halt at the foot of a gulch in a cloud of dust, its remaining wheels spinning aimlessly.

Ranger Archer, Tim and Chico reached the spot where it had gone over and peered down the almost perpendicular drop. 'Holy Mary! Chico hissed. 'I no like to take that ride.'

Archer took a small telescope from his pocket, put it to his eye and surveyed the wreckage. 'No sign of movement. Nobody ain't gonna get out of that alive.'

They stood and watched for a while. 'We'll go down and take a look later,' Archer decided.

Tim suddenly remembered the girl. 'Come on, we've got to get to Lucy.'

Buster Davis and three of the men had started down the trail on their broncs to see what had happened but came face to face with Archer as he led the charge up the narrow trail. 'Hold it!' he shouted, his revolver at the ready, cocked as he drew it from his right-hip holster. 'I'm the law. Hold it right there or we start shooting.'

There was barely a moment's hesitation on the part of the four. Most of their lives they had chosen to live by their own law, the law of the West, as Davis then displayed. 'A man don't step down for nobody.' His Smith & Wesson .44 spat lead before he leapt from his mustang and sought cover in the rocks of the cliffside.

They had three options: fight, surrender or turn tail and run. Maybe there was no point in fighting. Their boss was, by all probability, dead and they wouldn't get paid. But what the hell! 'You ain't taking me back to hang from that damn scaffold,' Rafe shouted, jumping from the saddle with his rifle in his hand and scrambling for safety.

Old Raker drew two saddle guns from within his long rain-cheater and met them head on, grim as a sentinel, peering from beneath the wide brim of his hat to let loose flame-flashing fire power from both barrels.

Archer went down, his pistols still firing, hit in the chest, thrown from his grey stallion to hug the ground. 'Don't let 'em get away, boys,' he coughed out.

Tim had to admit that his first thought was for the safety of his own valuable horse as he spun it around and sent it trotting away as he swung down beside the ranger. He knelt beside him and drew both Peacemakers, arms outstretched, gritting his teeth, his volley of lead blasting Raker from the saddle.

Chico ran up to join him. 'How is he?'

'I dunno. It don't look good.' Tim took a pot at a ginger-haired no-good in nondescript clothes, who returned fire, then swivelled his mustang in a cloud of dust and headed back up the trail.

Rusty was already nursing a forearm seared by Reuben's derringer and had no ambition for the fight. He made a run for freedom. His cowardice was rewarded by a slug in the back as Chico took careful aim with his carbine and brought him down. Rusty was dragged, bouncing along the rocky ground, his boot caught in his bentwood stirrup.

But Buster Davis and Rafe had achieved prime positions up on the hillside and were strafing their pursuers with a whistling and ricocheting fusillade. Chico and Tim kept their heads down, dragging the ranger into cover.

'They got us pinned down, *amigo*.'

'Yeah.' Tim was worried about the ranger who looked up at him with his steady grey eyes and forced out words. 'Don't bother about me. Get after 'em.'

'It's two against two now,' Tim said to Chico. 'I'll draw their lead while you get up behind 'em.'

'Hey, why me? Why not you?'

'OK, if you like.'

'No, I only joking.' He crossed himself as he waited for Tim to reload his revolvers. '*Adios, amigo.* Maybe we meet in the afterlife. Start shootin'.'

As Roberts did so, dashing forward up the trail to attract the fire of the two up in the rocks, Chico wriggled around a crevice which gradually opened wider into a chimney. He pressed his back against one wall and pushed himself upwards with his boots against the other wall. 'What I do now?' he asked as he reached a height of about thirty feet. 'I'm damn stuck.'

He spotted Rafe knelt behind a rock with his rifle, levering the Winchester and giving Tim trouble. He was so intent on the job he didn't see Chico stuck up in the chimney. Chico raised his carbine and took careful aim. 'Hey, take that!' he cried as his bullet caught Rafe in the side, twisted him and tossed him by the power of its velocity to go tumbling back down to the side of the trail. 'Good shootin',' Chico congratulated himself.

Buster Davis, wiping a drip of sweat from his

broken nose, turned to see where the bullet had come from and saw the Mexican in his big hat propped up between the cliff and a chimney of rock. 'You lousy greaser,' he growled. 'Say your prayers.'

'Aagh!' Chico cried, as he lost his footing and went slithering and sliding back down the chimney.

Davis's shot missed him by a hair's-breadth. 'Hot damn!' He shouted, anger surging to make him foolhardy. He climbed up on a rock to get a better view of the Mexican and presented Tim down below with a perfect target. His left-hand Peacemaker barked flame and death and Davis pitched forward to eat a mouthful of dust, his last meal on this earth.

Chico was groaning at his cuts and bruises, but he did not appear to have any broken bones. 'You're one lucky sonuvagun,' Tim said, helping him up.

'What's happened to them?'

'They're all dead. Come on, we got to go on up and find Lucy.'

When the wagon had pitched off the rimrock and Reuben Horovitz had been taken to certain death as it smashed on the rocks a thousand feet below, Lance Patterson had been thrown clear. He was sent tumbling down the start of the steep slope to become buried in a patch of cactus. He gathered his senses and was just about to extricate himself from the thorns when he heard the voices of three men up above.

Ranger Archer called out, 'We'll go down an' find the bodies later on.'

'That's what you think,' Lance groaned, needles sticking in his face, hair and hands, his suit torn and his nose bleeding from a lucky punch Reuben had got in. By the time he had managed to extricate himself from the cactus and hauled himself up hand over hand to the overhang, he had heard the fierce battle of guns begin.

He was by no means the dapper dude he had once been as he found a way up and crawled back on to the dusty trail. Indeed, he looked like he had been pulled through a hedge backwards, which in a way he had, a cactus hedge.

He looked up the trail and saw the gunfight in full swing. Why, he wondered, would his men keep fighting if they thought he was dead? Maybe it was just the instinct of cornered rats. But fight they did. If they thought he was dead ... the phrase repeated itself. Yes, why not let them think so? He would get out, disappear for a while.

He tried to pick the thorns from his face and hands as he ran off down the trail and caught hold of Buster Davis's mustang which had been sent bolting by the sound of the guns. He swung on to it and headed back towards River Bend, going as fast as the creature would go under whip and spur.

Suddenly Lance Patterson spotted a plume of dust kicked up by a band of riders and they were coming towards him along the winding trail. He pulled the mustang into hiding behind some giant rocks and watched Sheriff McBean and his posse of townsmen go thundering by.

Old Spanish customs died hard on this part of the frontier which not so long before had been part of the Mexican empire. About 1.30 p.m. most folks retired indoors for a light lunch followed by a siesta until about 4 p.m. when the stores reopened and the town came to life again.

River Bend was deathly quiet as Patterson rode in, just an occasional clatter of cutlery from inside the wooden frame or adobe houses. He wound the horse through the back alleys and reached the stable at the rear of the saloon. He peered through a back window and saw a few loiterers playing a desultory game of cards in one corner, the 'keep behind the bar polishing glasses.

He went up the back stairs and unlocked his door. 'Christ! What's happened here?' His expensively vulgar furnishings were in a mess as if hit by a bomb blast, and he gawped with surprise to see his safe door hanging from its hinges. He was even more surprised to see that some bundles of cash remained inside, although, when he counted it, it was severely depleted.

Lance went into the bedroom, changed into a

clean shirt and bow, pulled on fresh corduroy pants and a leather topcoat – he knew now why most range riders favoured buckskins! He washed his face of blood and combed back his hair, tossed a few articles into a carpet bag along with what cash remained, stuffed his Remington back in his leather belt and some cartridges in his pocket, and looked around him. Outside in the main street he could see the sturdy scaffold still waiting for its chosen victim.

'They ain't getting me on that,' he muttered. 'I'm getting out.'

He wanted to get away unseen on a fresh horse. But, as he headed for the back stairs, Darling Dolly let herself in from the saloon landing. 'Lance!' she exclaimed, closing the door behind her. 'I thought—'

'You thought I might be dead? Or arrested? You thought to see me swing high out there?' Lance put down his bag and strode towards her. 'What's been going on here? I've an idea you're behind it.'

'No,' she gurgled, hardly able to speak, as he caught her by the throat in a strong grip. 'I had nothing to do with it.'

'Oh, yeah? You ain't been helping yourself to my cash, I don't suppose? I wouldn't trust you further than I could spit. I oughta break your neck.'

For moments Dolly thought that was what he was going to do as he thrust her back against the wall and she felt her windpipe crack. His snarling face was up against hers; he was choking the life out of her. But then he threw her aside to stumble away on to the floor like a rag doll.

'So, who bust into the safe?'

'It was the sheriff,' she lied. 'He was looking for the map.' She soothed her throat as she choked the words out. 'They know all about you, Lance. They know it was you who murdered Crazy Ned.'

'Yeah, well, that's why I'm getting out.' Lance picked up his bag. 'But you can tell 'em I'll be back. And when I do it'll be with a vengeance. I'll burn this town down. And I'll kill anyone who tries to stop me.'

When he had gone, Dolly picked herself up and stood in a daze. 'You know, I think he means it,' she croaked. 'Me, I need a damn drink.'

'You an' me could git along fine, missy.' The dim-witted Randall had tied Lucy's wrists behind her and hitched the rope in a noose around her slim neck. 'We could make a break for it now, head for the border. Jest you an' me. Whadda ya say?'

Lucy wanted to say that the idea of being the concubine of such a sweaty, smelly, loathsome barrel of lard did not appeal one jot. But perhaps she could persuade him to release her? 'Perhaps. . . ?' she murmured.

He had taken her into the dark dusty cavern of the mine and now gave the rawhide rope a jerk so she was forced to move her body close to him. In

the dim light his ugly mug had the look of a plead-
ing gargoyle as he stared at her, maniacally. He had
never had much of a break, had seen the insides of
too many jails, but this time he had an idea this
pretty gal might fall for a big, virile guy like him.
She was certainly a nice bit of muslin that was for
sure.

'I could look after you, honey,' he drooled.
'Show you some good times.'

'Why don't you cut me loose,' she suggested,
'and go see what all that shooting's about?'

'Yuh?' Randall listened, his head cocked like a
dog. 'There's sure been one hell of a lot of
shootin'. Now it's gone quiet. Maybe the coast is
clear for us? But I ain't untying ya just yet.' He
grabbed her around the waist with his brawny left
arm and pushed her before him, brandishing his
six-gun with his right fist. 'I don't trust ya.'

As he spoke, Tim Roberts appeared in the arc of
the cavern doorway, his body silhouetted against
the harsh daylight. 'Keep back,' Lucy screamed.
'He's got a gun.'

'It's no use,' Tim shouted. 'Give yourself up. All
your pals are dead.'

'Yeah, an' you will be, too,' Randall mumbled, in
his thick-lipped way. 'I got the ace, buddy, the gal.'
He put the revolver to her temple. 'She gits her
brains splattered 'less you play it my way.'

'OK.' Tim spun his right-hand Peacemaker and
returned it to its holster. 'Don't do anything

stupid. I'm backing out.'

'Is that right? Lance an' t'others are gonners?'

'That's right. I'm the only one here. What do you want? I'll get you a horse and you can ride out.'

'What do I want? I want you outa the way.' The explosion of the gun in the enclosed space made Lucy scream with shock and fear as she saw Roberts collapse. The bullet had sledgehammered into his thigh.

Randall grinned, 'Take that, sucker.'

Tim grimaced with pain as he lay in the dust, blood trickling through his fingers as he held the wound. 'Right, cowboy.' Randall put the smoking revolver back to the girl's head as he edged hcr forward to peer down at him. 'Now, take them revolvers out nice an' easy an' toss 'em away if you want her to live. I ain't havin' you back-shootin' me.'

In spite of the nausea and dizziness spinning through him from the intensity of the pain, Roberts managed to do as Randall bid, skidding the revolvers away into the darkness. 'Why don't you leave her now?' he gritted out. 'Make a dash for it on your own. Don't be a fool. You take her you'll be hunted down.'

'Get lost, cripple.' Randall gave a hysterical giggle. 'She's comin' with me. She wants to, doncha, honey?'

He lowered the gun and pushed Lucy on out of

the mine. 'Hey, look, there's my hoss. We'll round up another, then we're outa here.'

'Hey *muchacho! que perro tan feo!* What an ugly dog, iss what I say.'

The Mexican's mocking voice made Randall spin around, confused. Chico was standing up above the mine entrance. He loosed a shot at him. Chico's Navy Colt barked out and the big man hurtled backwards to lay supine, a neat, bloody hole between his brows.

'Hey, what a dimbo. He no see me until it too late.' Chico sprang down and caught hold of Lucy. 'You all right?'

Lucy clung to him, gasping and shuddering as he loosed the rope, patted her back and soothed her. Then she extricated herself from his arms and ran back into the cave to kneel beside Tim. 'Don't worry,' she said. 'We'll get you out of here.'

'I'm OK,' he gasped. 'Tom Archer. He's bleeding bad from a chest wound. You better go see what you can do for him.'

'Yes.' She stared at him, nodding, seriously. 'I will.'

Just then there was a clatter of horses' hoofs and men shouting outside as Sheriff McBean's posse arrived. The overweight sheriff, rifle in his hands, pushed Chico before him into the cave. 'OK, you two. We've gotcha. You won't escape this time. We're gonna hang you high. Lucy! Thank God you're alive.'

'Oh, shut up, you fat fool,' she snapped. 'These two didn't kill my uncle. Why don't you go back to collecting fines?'

The sheriff stepped back, flummoxed, as she pushed him aside. 'There's no need to talk to me like that?' he whimpered. 'Who the hell did kill him then?'

'Lance Patterson.' Chico patted his shoulder. 'Why you look so sad? Maybe he a friend of yours. Maybe you theenk you get no more free drinks, free meals, free girls in his saloon no more? Meester, you theenk damn right.'

SEVEN

It was an uncanny sensation for Lance Patterson to be on the run, a hunted man, after his comfortable lifestyle running the Silver Cartwheel these past seven years with men and girls at his beck and call. How had things gone so disastrously wrong? If it hadn't been for that cowboy poking his nose in he would have been sitting pretty now. Not squatted down in the dirt fanning at a small fire trying to cook a cottontail rabbit he had shot.

Lance had taken the backtrails to try to avoid human contact. He didn't want to be seen just in case they had put out a murder warrant on him. 'Damn 'em all!' He cursed and coughed as smoke got in his throat and eyes. He wasn't used to this backwoodsman stuff, skinning and gutting the bloody thing and now waiting an age for it to roast. He was so hungry and exhausted he felt like biting into it raw.

'Yes, maybe it would be best to disappear,

change my name, start some place new,' he muttered through his swollen lips. 'Who would have thought that little rat would have packed such a punch? I was too confident all along the line. You can't underestimate people. I ain't gonna make the same mistake again.'

He was heading north to Tombstone, a hundred miles as the crow flies, but it would take him a good three days going this route through the hills. He had little water in his canteen either for himself or his horse, a flea-bitten grey with a spotted coat, the only fresh one he could find in the stable. He had begun to wonder if they would make it through. It was a harsh, bitter and unforgiving land, blasted by the heat of the sun, often hitting 120 degrees on the Fahrenheit scale. If a man sweated this much he needed plenty of water to cool the human engine. Lance had even tried picking some prickly pears, with difficulty, and sucking at their juice. It had added to the pains in his hands, knees and face from festering needles of the cacti.

'Goddamn it.' He cursed some more as he watched a red-tailed hawk hovering in the great expanse of sky. 'How did I get myself in this mess?'

The hawk suddenly swooped down to perch on a saguaro. What's he after? Lance wondered, and prowled nearer to get a better view. He could see the hawk's vicious curved beak, his talons gripping the pin cushion arm of the great cactus. Then he

saw the big diamondback rattler on the ground
seeming to sense the hawk. Kill or be killed, that
was the way of things out here. Lance watched,
entranced, as battle commenced. The hawk
hopped down and stood like some Mexican bull-
fighter, his wings outstretched tempting the snake
to strike. Suddenly he did so and the hawk leapt
into the air, narrowly to avoid the curved fangs.
The diamondback slid forward fast, making more
lightning strikes which the hawk avoided grace-
fully. It was almost impossible to follow the speed
of the snake's strikes. But the redtail was his match.
He leapt down from one jump to pinion the rattler
with his talons and tear at his head with his sharp
beak. Soon there was blood and the snake gave up
the struggle. The hawk looked about him, proudly
victorious. He saw the man and leapt away in to the
air, flying off, his supper dangling beneath him.

Lance went back to his own supper. The rabbit
was tough and rubbery, but he didn't care, burning his fingers as he held it, tearing at the flesh like
some aboriginal Indian. 'What wouldn't I pay for a
pint of Irish and a coffee?' he muttered, as he lay
back and watched the shadows of night closing in.
He shuddered at the prospect of one of those
diamondbacks slithering up to him as he slept. He
wrapped his saddle blanket around his legs for
some warmth for it got cold at night. He kept his
revolver ready-cocked in his belt, pulled his hat
over his eyes to cut out the glare of the rising

moon and tried to get some shut-eye. 'No, I won't make the same mistake again,' he whispered huskily before he finally succumbed to sleep.

His tongue was swollen in his mouth by the end of the second day when he reached the San Pedro river, an oasis of green amid the sun-dried chaparral. Patterson, at least, had the sense not to let his horse drink too much, but he threw himself down head first and wallowed in the cool freshness of the water. Suddenly Lance froze as he heard mocking laughter and saw the shadows of the horsemen standing over him.

'What we got here, boys, a fish or a man?' an American voice drawled, while there was the shrill parrot-like Spanish chatter of two of his companions. Lance slowly looked up and what he saw he did not like. A band of twenty or so *viciosos*, in greasy leathers, packing iron, and strung with bandoliers of bullets; they looked twice as vicious as those dregs of the frontier he had employed back at the saloon: a pack of wild dogs.

'A poor weary traveller,' one of the Mexicans giggled, gold flashing in his mouth. 'I wonder if he pack many dollars for us?'

'His nag certainly ain't worth much.' The sawtooth drawl of a young American, flashily attired in black silk shirt, black pants and silver-toed boots, signified he was from the south. 'But you cain't allus tell by appearances.'

Lance wearily got to his feet in the small space allowed him by the men on horseback. They seemed to have appeared out of nowhere. 'Boys,' he said, brushing himself down. 'It wouldn't be advisable to rob me.'

The young one, named Johnny Ringo, showed a flash of white teeth as he smiled down at him. 'Why not?'

'Because I'm on your side. I'm one of you.' He offered his dripping wet hand. 'Lance Patterson. I run the saloon an' whorehouse at River Bend. I could put business your way.'

Ringo ignored his hand and glanced across at a more surly, unkempt character, who was watching him through muddy eyes. Ike Clanton was the leader of their band now that Old Man Clanton had been killed on a rustling expedition into Mexico. 'Hear that, Ike? This saloon-keep's advisin' us not to rob him. He's got the gall to suggest he might employ *us*.'

'I heard him,' Ike growled. 'Let's see what he's got on him first.'

'You see we ain't had a very successful trip this time.' Johnny Ringo stepped down and relieved Lance of his Remington. 'Some *federales* took exception to us stealing some Mex beeves. We had to hightail it back fast to this side of the border.'

Lance eyed the bunch of thugs sitting their horses, fingering the triggers of their weapons as if impatient to shoot him down, and knew there was little point in arguing. So he opened his leather coat and let Johnny Ringo frisk him.

'Well, whadda ya know?' Ringo hollered, pulling out wads of cash. 'The saloon-keep's a wealthy man.' He tossed the bundles to Clanton. 'Seems like it's our lucky day, after all, boys. Who'da thought we'd come across this ripe chicken ready to be plucked.'

Ike Clanton flicked through the greenbacks and shrugged. 'Why you carryin' all this dough, mister? You on the run?'

'It's a long story,' Lance replied. 'Why don't I come back with you to wherever you're staying tonight and I'll explain the situation. I can assure you this stuff is peanuts to the cash I could put your way.'

'What'n hell you talkin' about?'

'A mine. We could take it over. I could – with your help. It's—'

'We ain't miners,' Clanton rapped out, turning his horse away. 'Kill the crazy 'coon.'

The *viciosos* began to draw their handguns, grinning and ready. This was going to be a joint execution. Lance licked his dry lips and screamed, 'You fool! That mine's worth a fortune.'

Ike reined in and turned back. 'What did he call me? You want me to hand you over to Indian Joe first, mister? You wouldn't like what he does.'

'I said,' Lance protested, 'you're turning your back on a fortune if you kill me. I can make you rich.'

Ike Clanton's eyes were like hard jewels beneath his shaggy brows, but suddenly they gleamed with greed. 'Bring the saloon-keeper along,' he said. 'We'll give him a chance to say his piece.'

It was mid-afternoon a week later as Tim Roberts lay on the bed and watched Lucy tidying the bedroom. The only sound was the buzzing of a fly and the rustle of her candy-stripe dress. She was a busy little body seeming to take everything in her stride. She had spent days clearing out Ned's cabin, sweeping the floorboards, whitewashing the walls, burning his dirty old bedding, wiping away the grease and cobwebs, tidying the wood around the stove. She had ordered two new palliases to be sent out from the town store, covered them with clean sheets and blankets, insisted that Tim take one bunk and she the other.

'You're always on the go,' he said. 'It makes me me feel kinda useless just lying here.'

'You're awake?' She glanced at him. 'I thought you'd dozed off.' Lucy came and sat beside him on his bunk. 'You've got to have patience, Tim. The doc said you'd be on your feet in two weeks and be able to walk without crutches after another two. You're doing pretty well.'

'Yes, I guess so, but I ain't used to being on my backside all day. How's Tom?'

'He's doing fine.' Lucy had just returned from visiting the Archer place.' He reckons that you and him are both lucky to be alive and I agree with him.'

'True, I s'pose. Coulda lost my leg if gangrene had set in. Many a man has.' Tim reached out and held her hand. 'I owe it all to you. You're a damn fine nurse.'

'And I'm still around because you and Chico turned up.' Her bright violet eyes met his. 'So we're quits, I guess.'

The posse had found a stand of pines which had found nourishment in the stark landscape, cut boughs and stretchered him and Archer down the mountainside. It had been a gruelling journey. They had both lost a lot of blood. When they reached Ned's ranch house she had told him that he could stay with her until he recovered. He had passed out at that point and come to some time later, his leg in splints and a concerned Lucy dabbing at his brow.

After she had made him comfortable, Lucy had told him she was catching the stage to Bisbee and he would have to fend for himself until she got back the next day. It was like the lonesome cabin was suddenly filled with sunshine when she returned. 'I've registered the mine in my name,' she announced, her eyes bright, as she fed him some soup.

'That's good.'

'And in yours. Don't argue. Eat your bread and broth like a good boy.'

'What are you talking about?' he expostulated, spilling a mouthful. 'Why in my—'

'Because Uncle Ned told me he liked and trusted you. You were the right stuff. That's what he said. And he told me that he had offered to take you into partnership. So I've got to honour his word.'

Since then she had nursed him and attended to his needs, between putting up gingham curtains at the windows, carpets on the floorboards, covering the table with a cloth and arranging plates and new pots in the kitchen, generally brightening the old place up.

'You act like you're planning to stay,' Tim said. 'Ain't you planning on going back to Tombstone?'

'Well, I guess I'll have to soon as you can get out of bed. I'll have to tell Pa about everything. A pity he, or you, couldn't have come to Uncle Ned's service but it was a bit of a rush job on account of the heat. I'm planning on getting him a real nice headstone for his grave down by the stream.'

Lucy went to the kitchen to fetch some hot water in a basin with cotton wool and sat back beside him. 'Now come on, pull your pants down. I got to take a look at the wound.' She pulled back the bedclothes and changed the dressing. 'Yes, it's coming on fine considering how that bullet smashed through bone, nerves and blood vessels. It's truly amazing how the body can heal itself.'

'With a little help from people like you,' Tim

said. 'I dunno how I'm ever gonna repay you.'

'I'll think of a way.' She put the bowl aside and smiled at him, stroking fingers down his good thigh. 'You've got real nice legs, muscled, I guess, from all that horse-riding.'

'Hey, don't,' he said, pulling up the sheet. He sighed. 'Dunno whether I'll ever be able to race Brandy again.'

'Sure you will.' She ran her fingers up to his hip, left them lingering there, tantalizingly. 'You were damn lucky that bullet wasn't three inches higher.'

'Yeah,' Tim agreed, 'It coulda ruined my marital prospects.'

Lucy giggled and moved her hip in on to the bed, so she could stretch out more comfortably next to him. 'So you figure on having marital prospects, do you?'

'Sure. Why not? Most guys do.'

'You don't have anybody particular in mind, I suppose?' Lucy's face was close to his. 'Go on, don't be shy. You can tell me.'

Tim swallowed his alarm. It was the closest he had ever been to the girl. She had never lain on his bed like this before. They were practically body to body, although admittedly she was clothed and outside the covers. Normally she would string a sheet between their two bunks before she retired to bed and call out a sisterly goodnight.

'Look, Lucy, I'm just a cowboy who drifts like the tumbling tumbleweed. You said so yourself. I've no right to proposition the daughter of a wealthy storekeeper. Hang it, I'm skint. What can—'

Lucy butted in. 'You *are* wealthy, lunkhead. Hasn't it sunk in yet? You have half-ownership of a mine. Or you will have once you get off your butt and start working at it. And then—'

'Then what?'

'It ain't leap year, Tim. I can't ask you.'

'You mean?' he put an arm around her, drew her to him and kissed her lips. 'You mean you would?'

'Of course I would,' she murmured, as her fingers fluttered upwards beneath the sheet. 'No, you definitely haven't lost your marital prospects!'

'Yeah.' His cheek dimpled as he grinned at her. 'I do believe I've come back to life.'

Meanwhile Chico had moved in with Darling Dolly, who had decided to keep on running the Silver Cartwheel in Lance's absence. In fact, she had decided not to mention that he was still alive and kicking. She generally sat at the bar and kept an eye on things just the way she had done before and kept an account book of income and expenditure, giving herself a raise she was long overdue, and taking only a twenty-five per cent cut of the girls' takings, instead of the seventy-five that Lance would pocket. She had continued to order cartloads of whiskey and steam beer from the teamsters, plus other necessities like candles and kitchen supplies, and had spent part of the takings in refurbishing the top room, its previous furnishings wrecked by her safe-blowing activities. Everything was rolling along fine and dandy. Business was booming as miners, hearing of Ned's lucky strike, arrived to try their own luck in the hills.

'Who needs Lance Patterson?' she asked, as she took a siesta with Chico in Lance's bed. Her only problem was keeping the cheeky Mexican's amorous hands off the other girls. So, she made sure she kept him sweet with plenty of loving.

That afternoon Chico was lying back languidly and telling Dolly about his poverty-stricken childhood. 'I lost my daddy early in life,' he said, dolefully. 'Mama and I saw him fall down a hole and die.'

'What,' Dolly murmured, 'an empty well or something?'

'No, a gallows. He drop through, what you say, trapdoor? He was hanged. All he done was shoot a man.' He gave a bellow of a laugh. 'Hey, who cares? My mama, and me we get on fine without him.'

Dolly looked out of the window, apprehensively, at the sturdy gallows that had been left standing in the street. 'I wish they'd demolish that damn thing.'

'They wait for next customer. We cheat them of their fun, my cactus flower.' He kissed her hand.

'You save my life.'

'Yes,' Dolly breathed in his ear, wriggling her ageing, half-naked body into his. It was as if she could never get enough of him. 'Let's do it again, sweetheart, before the flowers wither and droop.'

'*Sí*, you may be scraggy ol' cheeken but I like you better than any other gal I ever met.'

'You say the sweetest things.'

By the time Tim had begun to struggle up on to his crutches and hop around, Lucy had employed a trustworthy Latino as labourer at the mine, purchased timber props, drills, sledgehammers, a wagon, horses, and dynamite, and started her team shovelling and digging. Uncle Ned had already got enough ore out for a load, so they had taken it to Bisbee and got a good price. Lucy was elated as she showed Tim the cheque.

In the mornings they – she, Tim, Chico and Manuel – would drive up on the wagon to the mine.

The cowboy was mighty impressed by the way she had fenced off the area with barbed wire and erected a big sign stating, Latigo Canyon Mining Company – proprietors, Tim and Lucy Roberts.'

She hugged his arm. 'I know it looks like I'm jumping the gun a bit. We ain't married yet but we soon will be once Daddy gives his consent. So we might as well get ready for the big event.'

Tim hobbled into the mine to take a look and

was again impressed by all the equipment and all the work already done. But the shaft only went twenty feet into the hill before it reached a solid wall of rock. 'Where'n hell do we go now?' He tipped his hat over his eyes and scratched the back of his head as Lucy held up the lantern. 'I don't know nothing about mining. Cows is all I know,' Tim said. 'We need to get expert advice. Mining is notoriously dangerous work. Thousands have been killed and maimed from not knowing what the hell they're playing at.'

'That's all right. I bought a book about deep mining in Bisbee. I've been swotting up. Apparently it's best to dig down at an angle and come up under the seam. That way, once you've drilled up into it, the ore can be hacked out and dropped down into tubs by gravity.'

'Hmm?' Tim muttered, dubiously. 'How you gonna haul it up, then?'

'Easy. Manuel's promised to sell me – I mean, us – four mules. They'll do the hard work.'

'You've certainly got it all figured out.'

'Come on, Tim. Be more encouraging. Don't you want to be rich?'

'To tell you the truth, gal, I ain't sure that I do if it means spending my life down in this dark, silent hole. It gives me the creeps. Let's get out of here.'

When they emerged into the sunlight Lucy smiled. 'You gotta look on the bright side, Tim.

106

We're in this together now. I've spent a lot of money on equipment. We've got to see a return.'

Tim nodded, thoughtfully. 'Yeah, OK. I guess I'll give it a go.'

EIGHT

The gang of rustlers had been at their hideout for a couple of weeks, playing cards and idling. Ike Clanton had gone on a massive drunk, staggering around, cursing, shouting, firing his pistols, and he warned Lance that if he tried to escape he would shoot him. So he was forced to keep his head down and kick his heels with the rest of them holed up at the run-down ranch on the western slopes of the Dragoons. By now Lance Patterson realized he would have to act with some authority if he were to get this bunch of morons on his side, or, at the very least, persuade them not to murder him.

'You boys been thinkin' over my offer?' he asked one night as the majority of the gang tumbled into the bunkhouse and began stoking up the tin stove and flopping out. 'It would be an easy life. All you'd have to do would be hang around my mine and shoot any varmint who caused me trouble. I'd pay you well. You could relax at my saloon, wimmin and booze on the house.'

The big one, Curly Bill Brocius, his gimlet eyes peering through a tangle of hair and beard, lit a cheroot and growled, 'Sounds int'restin', pal. You'd better beat it out with Ike. We got thangs to do in Tombstone first.'

They were an oddly assorted bunch, the sharply dressed, clean-shaven Johnny Ringo; a horse-thief called Pony Deal; the scar-faced Florentino 'Indian Charlie' Cruz; a couple of hard-faced hold-up men, Hank Swilling and Frank Stillwell, who also acted as deputy sheriff at Tombstone, and the Mex *bandidos* with their evil, taunting grins.

'You look like the ideal kinda bunch I need,' Lance announced, as he watched them stuffing their bellies from tin plates piled with 'sonuvabitch stew', plaguing the Mexican woman cook, or sprawling back, lighting up and passing a jug of corn whiskey. 'We could take over River Bend, make it our town. The lawman's already in my pocket.'

'C'mon,' Johnny Ringo drawled. 'Let's talk it over with Ike, if he ain't got too much of a hang-over.'

They left the noisy hullabaloo of the bunkhouse, followed by Frank, who had not been on the rustling expedition but ridden the thirty-five miles out from Tombstone that day. His badge was openly displayed on his shirt as if he didn't give a damn whose company he kept.

They sauntered past the corrals, flooded now by the silver of a rising moon, illuminating the stark landscape all around. Lance felt a strange excitement as they spur-clattered into the ranch house, sensing that the odds might well turn again to his advantage.

The rancher, Pete Spencer, had his boots up, a jug of coffee and used plates on the kitchen table. Ike Clanton was sat in a rocker, his face malign and sour. His younger brother, Phin, was watching him.

Since the shoot-out at the OK Corral when his other teenage brother, Billy, had gone down, gun blazing, taken out, along with two other members of the gang, by the more accurate shooting of Marshal Wyatt Earp and his brothers, and his side-kick, Doc Holliday, Ike Clanton had been obsessed with thoughts of revenge.

'Whadda ya want?' he shouted, not caring to have these thoughts disturbed.

Maybe it was guilt, the memory of his own cowardice that tormented him. He, himself, had thrown up his hands, begged for mercy from Earp and run off for safety, leaving Billy to bite the dust.

Ike Clanton had always been a coward, preferring to backshoot a man in the dark rather than face him. Three times he had taken the insults of Holliday and refused to fight. There had been bad blood between the inbred, hillbilly Clanton clan and the more sophisticated Earp family since the day the latter had arrived. Before that the Clantons had always ruled the roost in Tombstone and Cochise county.

'It seems to me this bozo is talking some sense, Ike,' Johnny Ringo said, nodding at Lance Patterson. 'Maybe we oughta investigate his offer.'

'I got things on my mind,' Clanton growled. 'I ain't got time for no other operation until Earp and his brothers pay for murderin' poor Billy. You know that.'

'Sure I know it, Ike.' Johnny Ringo had the swagger of a professional shootist, but Wyatt Earp was not a man he would care to face, himself. 'We'll get 'em soon enough.'

'We'll get 'em tomorrow. Pete here has come up with a plan. We'll do the same as we did to Virgil, shotgun 'em. We'll wait until it gets dark and they ain't expectin' us. It's time for another showdown.'

'Who exactly do you mean by we?' Ringo asked, nervously, chewing on a slim cheroot.

Ike had been counting Lance Patterson's wads of greenbacks, totalling a thousand dollars, and slapped them down in three piles on the table. 'This'll go to those who do it. Pete here has volunteered. We need two more.'

'Count me out,' Ringo said. 'It ain't my kinda operation.'

'Count me in.' Deputy Stillwell's eyes gleamed greedily as he saw the piles of dollars. 'Nobody will suspect me. Sheriff Behan will back us up.'

'Who else?' Clanton muttered. 'I can't. It would be too obvious. It's gotta be somebody with no particular grudge.'

'How about Indian Charlie?' Ringo suggested. 'He would kill anybody. No need to pay him that much. Give him twenty-five bucks.'

'Go get him,' Clanton ordered, his dark eyes turning to Lance. 'How about you, saloon-keep? You willing to prove you're one of us?'

Lance looked a trifle startled. 'Howja mean?'

'Nobody knows you in Tombstone. You ride into town and find out where Earp is. Then you tip the others off.'

If he didn't agree, it occurred to Lance, no doubt his suggested deal would be off. There was no real danger for him in it. 'OK, I'll do it. If I do, you'll—?

'We'll talk about it. Here, you better have some of your cash back.' Ike handed him $200 from Indian Charlie's share. 'You'll need to buy a few drinks, look around the saloons for the Earps, get yourself a hotel.'

So, Lance thought, when he went back to the bunkhouse, I'm being paid with my own money to take part in the attempted assassination of one of the most feared shootists on the frontier. Am I going crazy? Or what?

112

*

Now that she had the mine up and running and Tim was on his feet, albeit on crutches, Lucy decided it was time to take the stage to Tombstone to announce her engagement to her widower father, and tell him she couldn't work as his chief cashier any more as she was going into business on her own. She wanted to do things decent, have a church wedding and, she hoped, he would see that Tim was the right man for her.

She was waiting outside the Wells Fargo office at River Bend when she spotted the sheriff passing by. Lucy cornered him, angrily. 'Mr McBean, I'd like to know why you haven't issued any Wanted posters on Lance Patterson for the murder of my Uncle Ned?'

McBean hitched up his gunbelt as best he could around his ample belly and frowned at her. 'Lance died in that wagon crash. We all know that. Maybe his body ain't been found, but it probably tumbled down into some rocky crevice. You'll see, some-body'll come across his skeleton one day.'

'What if he isn't dead?'

'Waal . . .' McBean scratched his head, 'let's face it, there ain't any real evidence that he did kill Ned. Nobody saw him at the scene.'

'But he stole his wallet. It must have been—'

'No must about it. It's all circumstantial. Nobody would convict him on that.'

'Circumstantial, my eye. It's my opinion you were on his side.'

McBean wagged a finger at the girl. 'Don't you come the Miss Bossy Britches with me or it's you who will be in the hoosegow for contempt.'

'Contempt of what – you?'

'Don't you go round talking like that or I'll have you locked up right now.'

'You dare try!'

Lucy stared at the sheriff indignantly, waving her parasol, but fortunately the four-horse stage rolled in right then in a cloud of dust so the confrontation came to an end. 'Arrest me? Huh!' she exclaimed as she settled herself in the coach. 'It's him who should be arrested.'

By changing horses at the various stage stations along the route and travelling on through the night, the hundred-mile journey to Tombstone was completed by the next morning. Lucy felt like a pea that had been shaken in a colander for twenty-four hours as she stepped down and claimed her bag.

'Hi, Miss Lucy, you been away? I thought I hadn't seen your smiling face in the store,' a voice drawled. 'May I help you with that?'

The man who spoke was more than six feet tall, thin as a whip, wearing a frock-coat suit of Victorian black, white linen and string bow tie. He touched a finger to the brim of his black hat, his eyes beneath grey and steady as stones.

'Hello, Wyatt. Yes, I'd be glad of a hand. I've a few bundles I've bought as presents for Dad. Hi, Morgan, how are you?'

'I'm fine, Lucy.' Although dressed in a similar manner and sporting, like Wyatt, a heavy moustache, the fashion of the time, Morgan was more handsome than his severe older brother, and gave her a boyish grin as he picked up a parcel. 'Hey, what you got in here, a gold nugget? It weighs a ton.'

'No, it's silver. It's from my mine. I brought it to show Dad in case he doesn't believe me.'

'Your mine?' Morgan yelled. '*I* don't believe you.'

'Well, it was really Uncle Ned's but he got murdered. Now it belongs to me and my fiancé.'

'Your fiancé?' Morgan looked taken aback for at one time he had stepped out with Lucy and had had high hopes. But she had turned him down. 'This is sudden, ain't it?'

'Maybe, but it's the real thing.' As they walked across Tombstone's wide main street she filled them in on what had happened in River Bend, how she had been kidnapped by the murderer of her uncle, vilely assaulted, but rescued from his clutches. 'Oh, my golly gosh!' she suddenly cried, pointing a finger. 'There he is! The very man!'

Wyatt and Morgan looked across the street and

saw Lance Patterson stepping down from his fleabitten grey. 'Are you sure? I ain't seen him before,' Wyatt murmured, 'nor no Wanted bills on him.'

'No, the sheriff down there says there's no real evidence, only mine and Tim's. The cheek of it! He ought to be in jail.'

'Oh, another sheriff like Behan,' Morgan said, 'We know the kind.'

'Just a minute,' Wyatt shouted, as he strode across the wide road, drew his revolver, spun Lance around by the shoulder and pistol-whipped him across the jaw.

Patterson fell, sprawled in the dust, spat blood and a loosened tooth out, and cried, 'What was that for?'

'A present from a young lady. I've heard how you murdered her uncle and molested her. If you ever go near her again it will be the last thing you ever do, mister.'

'Who the hell are you?'

'My name's Earp. Remember it. If you ever want to try me you'll find me in the Oriental Saloon. OK?'

'So that's him,' Lance hissed as he watched the tall man turn his back and walk back deliberately to Morgan and Lucy standing outside the empor-ium. 'I may just find you sooner than you think, pal.'

A burly, curly-haired man with an Irish brogue,

bent to help Lance to his feet. 'What the divil's goin' on?'

'Beats me.' Lance waggled his jaw, glad that although it hurt like hell it wasn't broken. 'Ain't got a clue. Never seen him before. He just came up and hit me.'

'I'm the town sheriff here, John Behan.' He tapped the tin star on his suit lapel and scowled across at the Earps. 'It's time those mad dogs were put down.'

'That's just what I was thinking,' Lance agreed, eyeing the big man, shiftily. 'So you're Behan?'

There had been no love lost between Sheriff Behan and Wyatt since the Earp brothers, with their wives, had arrived in Tombstone two years before and bought themselves fancy frame houses with gardens and porches. Wyatt had made $30,000 on a mining deal and moved in on the Oriental Saloon and Gambling Hall, demanding a fighting share, as he called it, a quarter of the profits. And his brother Virgil was elected town marshal in direct opposition to Behan. Basically it was a battle between the two gangs fighting for the major share of the legal and lucrative liquor, gaming and prostitution business in Tombstone.

Soon Wyatt had sent for Bat Masterson, Luke Short and Doc Holliday, three of the most renowned gunfighters on the frontier, to join him as dealers and help part the miners from their hard-earned cash in games of faro, poker, monte and around the roulette wheel. The gaming hell was open night and day. There were scales on the tables: most transactions were counted out in gold dust or silver.

All the loud-mouthed, blustering Behan could do was congregate with his Clanton cronies in the less-prosperous Alamo across the street and plot the Earps' downfall. His hatred was fuelled by the fact that Wyatt had 'stolen' his long-term mistress, the raven-haired Josephine Marcus, from him. Whenever he saw them together it was like a red rag to a bull.

First Sheriff Behan tried to have the Earps arrested for the hold-up of a Wells Fargo stage, carrying a cargo of $26,000, in which the driver and a passenger were killed, even though the Clantons were the chief suspects.

Then, when Deputy Sheriff Frank Stillwell and small-time rancher Pete Spence robbed the Bisbee coach he tried again to place the blame on the Earps.

Whenever the Clanton gang arrived in town to get drunk and paint it red, one incident led to another. Even when Curly Bill Brocius wildly killed another city marshal, Jim White, and Wyatt disarmed and arrested him, the murderer was not in jail for long. Sheriff Behan persuaded the judge to deem it an accident and he was released with a reprimand.

Thus matters reached an explosive head when on 26 October, 1881, Wyatt, his brothers Virgil and Morgan, and Doc Holliday, loosened their shooting irons and set off down Fremont Street, their funereal coats billowing in the breeze to answer a challenge from the Clanton gang. They found them waiting at the OK Corral. Thirty seconds of gun-blazing violence left young Billy and two of Clanton's sidekicks dead in the dust.

Tombstone's two newspapers were strongly split by the duel. *The Nugget* trumpeted that the Earps should be arraigned for murder. But the rival *Epitaph* under its banner headline GUNFIGHT AT THE OK CORRAL claimed that it had been a fair fight.

'You shoulda shot that sonuvabitch Ike Clanton months ago,' Doc Holliday told Wyatt and Morgan, when they entered the Oriental and joined him at the poker table. 'It woulda saved us all a lot of trouble. The same goes for that bastard Behan.'

Wyatt, as always, was poker-faced and dour, a man with little if any sense of humour. 'I don't shoot a man in the back if he throws down his gun and runs like that coward Clanton did. Nor do I think it would be advisable to kill the town sheriff unless he draws first.'

'Please yourself.' Doc's profession was a dentist, but he had drilled more men than teeth. His eyes were luminous, his body racked by consumption.

119

He knew he was dying and had turned to the bottle for consolation. He had already started on his first of the day. He dealt the cards and drawled, 'You're too much of a gentleman, Wyatt. Scum like them don't deserve consideration.'

'Aw, we ain't scared of 'em,' young Morgan grinned, although he had been badly hurt in the shoot-out at the corral, hit in the base of the neck by a bullet. 'They know better than to trouble us again.'

'I wouldn't be too sure of that, Morgan,' his brother Virgil muttered. 'Look what they done to me. Maybe it's time we got outa Tombstone 'fore it becomes our tombstone.'

The memory of that dark Christmas-season night flashed into his mind, as it so often did; that midnight when he had left the Oriental and had become framed in the light from the Eagle Brewery saloon. Five shotguns had blasted out and town marshal Virgil Earp went down scattered with buckshot. He had been crippled for life, and now had to hobble around on crutches.

Ike Clanton, Johnny Ringo, Frank Stillwell, and Hank Swilling were witnessed running away, smoking shotguns in their hands. But when they were arrested and charged they claimed to have been miles away that night. For some reason the witnesses suddenly changed their minds and agreed this must have been so.

'It's no use being bitter, Virgil.' Wyatt studied his

hand. 'At least you're alive. Nobody's running me outa town.'

Wyatt had his own problems. His first wife, Irilla, had died of typhoid. He had got so mad drunk that night he had burned down their house. He had never touched anything stronger than coffee since. His second wife, Mattie, was a hopeless laudanum addict and off her head, which was why he had taken up with Josephine.

'Hey,' he said, flicking out a card, 'young Lucy over at the emporium's holding an engagement party tonight. She's invited me an' Morgan along. You wanna join us, Virgil?'

'Maybe,' muttered Virgil, morosely, 'I'll see you. there.'

Suddenly, from the far end of the spacious gaming emporium came the rap of an explosion followed in quick succession by another barking out and the crash of furniture as a bearded miner was propelled backwards to collapse on the floor.

'What'n hell . . .' Wyatt muttered, as he strode over to investigate, 'is going on here, Bat?'

But it was obvious what had happened as a pool of vivid red blood began to curdle across the boards. The acrid scent of gunsmoke drifted as his dealer, Masterson, returned his revolver to its holster. 'This bozo got fresh. I had to plug the sonuvabitch.'

'It was a fair fight,' a man shouted, as others

nodded agreement. 'Jake drew first. He got all hot under the collar about losing his stake.'

'Well, he's cooling fast now.' Wyatt beckoned to the barkeep. 'Get this stiff over to the under-taker's. He's messing up the floor. OK, men, you can get back to your games. It's all over.'

When the miner's corpse had been hauled out by its bootheels, Wyatt drawled, 'Come on, Bat. This ain't a good start for the day. We don't want Sheriff Behan trying to arrest us.'

'Let him try,' Masterson growled, tipping his bowler jauntily over one eye. 'This guy had the nerve to suggest I was dealin' from the bottom of the pack.' His broad face split into a beaming grin as he reshuffled the deck and, with the same light-ning speed and precision that he used a gun, spread out four aces on to the table. 'Did they come from the bottom? No, from several parts of it. I got a good memory, thassall.'

'Yeah, well, try to keep the punters sweet.' Earp slapped Bat's shoulder. 'Let 'em win now and again. We can't afford any more trouble. I've got an uneasy feeling in me today.'

Morgan never made it to Lucy's party. That night Wyatt suggested they play awhile first in the Campbell and Hatch billiards parlour on Allen Street before strolling along. Suddenly, as Morgan bent down over the table, two shots were fired from outside crashing through the window of the lighted saloon. Both slugs powered through

Morgan's back. A third shot whistled past Wyatt's head. He pulled out his revolver as he ducked down and returned fire. But by the time he got outside the assassins were gone.

Wyatt returned and cradled his favourite brother in his arms as he died slowly in agony. 'I'm going to get them for you, Morgan,' he whispered. 'I swear to you.'

NINE

Sweat trickled rivulets through the grey dust plastering Chico's face and body as he swung the eight-pound sledge upwards to hit the three-foot-long steel held by his fellow Mexican, Manuel. He cursed as the sweat got in his eyes and he missed, and stepped back to take a breather after twenty blows.

'Thees ees hellish work,' he gasped. 'What am I doin' here? I theenk I go back to Me-hico.'

'Yeah, men must have great greed to spend their lives down dark holes like this.' Tim still had splints on his leg and needed a stick to hop about. He felt guilty about not being able to help as he watched the operation. 'Gold fever I guess they call it. Or silver fever.'

It had taken three days of back-breaking work to hack into the solid rock and extend the tunnel downwards under the main seam, rock so hard they had to take the steel chisels into the black-

124

smith to be sharpened every day. They had been working for an hour attempting to make this drill hole in the rock above them and it was still only about two feet in length.

'We need to go another six inches,' the grey-haired Manuel said, as he relieved Chico of the sledge to take his turn, 'before we put in the dynamite.'

'Why do you do this, old man?' Chico asked, reinserting the steel drill. 'Can you not find other work?'

'No.' Manuel hefted the hammer with a grimace. 'I have many mouths to feed.'

'*Sí*, so I noticed.' When he had visited Manuel's *casa* to collect the mules he had met his wife. She had three children hanging around her legs, one sucking at her breast and, by the look of her beily, another on the way. 'That is why I never want to get married. It must be like a great weight around your neck. Me, I find 'em, use 'em and forget 'em.'

'Many a man has made that proud boast,' Tim smiled, 'and ended up in front of the altar.'

'Oh, no, just because you will be standing there tomorrow with me as your best man, don't think I will be fool enough to follow you. Come on, Manuel, give it another try.'

As Tim watched the older man struggling to smash the heavy sledge upwards to hit the steel he did wonder why a man like him had so many offspring. Maybe it was because he had nothing else to do at night? On the other hand, he thought, to have a family must be very fulfilling, as well as fun – if a man could afford it. No, he would not like to be like Chico. He thanked his lucky stars he had found a fine girl to love.

'That should about do it,' Chico said, as they took another break. 'We can stick the dynamite in now.'

'Thank the Lord for Alfred Nobel!'

'Who ees he?'

'The Swedish scientist who invented this stuff.' Tim handed Chico a stick. 'Now it is safe to handle. Before they used black powder. That was dangerous enough, but nitroglycerine's a million times worse. So sensitive just the sound of the human voice can set it off. There wouldn't be much left of a man if it did blow.'

'How you know all this?'

'Lucy's been reading it to me. Mining ain't for amateurs. There's so much precision work involved, so much to know.'

'So, how you know we doin' this right?'

'This is the easy bit.' The first stick of dynamite had been stuffed to the end of the hole and its percussion cap attached. Tim handed Chico another. And then a third. They had made three holes in this roof of the cavern in a triangle and angled to meet at the apex of a pyramid within the rock. 'Hauling the stuff out is *really* gonna make you sweat.'

'Yeah, *amigo*, you lucky sonuvagun you got that broken leg and don't have to help.'

Tim took a look at the 'rats'-tails' dangling down. 'That's fine. OK, boys, time to hightail it out of here while I light the fuses.'

'Careful with those blasting caps,' Manuel warned Chico in Spanish. 'I knew a man put them in his pocket and they got mixed in his tobacco. When he lit his pipe – boom! He lost his nose.'

'You don' say?' Chico hastily put them back into a box. 'I am very fond of my nose. I don' wanna lose it.'

They climbed back out of the cave and waited for Tim to emerge. 'He take a long time,' Chico said, anxiously.

'Maybe he wants to make sure they all catch.'

Tim scrambled out, leaning on his crutch. 'Here it goes, boys.'

There was the roar and rumble of a muffled explosion and a cloud of dust spurted out of the hole in the bare, egg-shaped hill. '*Olé*!' Manuel gave a yell of triumph and immediately headed back in.

'Wait a minute!' Tim shouted, 'Just in case—'

His face tensed as he caught hold of Chico to hold him back and they heard another rumble and clatter of rocks, more dust billowing out. 'Oh, Jesus!'

It took an hour to dig out the old man from the rubble. His dark face had blanched beneath the dust and was strained in agony. He gasped with pain as they hauled him out into the sunshine. 'It's my back,' he groaned. 'My legs. I have no feeling in them.'

'Oh, Lord!' Tim moaned again as he knelt beside him and dabbed water from his canteen on to his parched lips. 'Chico, you better ride into town, get the doc. We'll have to stretcher him down the hill by the look of it.'

When Chico had raced away on Satan, Tim tried to comfort Manuel but the old man's face was grim. 'What if I cannot work any more?' he asked, pleadingly. 'My family will starve.'

'Don't worry,' Tim tried to reassure him. 'You'll be OK.'

But as he got to his feet he was not so sure. Up in the sky a turkey vulture was slowly circling as if it had already sensed prey. Tim looked around at the sun-blasted rocks. There was an emptiness here like the void. 'I've had a feelling all along,' he said to himself, 'that this damn mine was going to be bad luck.'

The surly, curly-haired Irishman, Sheriff Behan, stood in the doorway of his office and watched the whole Earp family, wives and children, led by Wyatt, the crippled Virgil, and the youngest brother, Warren, accompany the coffin of Morgan along the wide and dusty Tombstone street to the spanking new railroad terminus. They were all in wind-flapping funereal black.

'Look like a bunch of scraggy crows, don't they?' his deputy, Frank Stillwell, scoffed.

'Looks to me like they've finally had enough,' Behan remarked, taking a chaw of a plug of baccy. 'They're clearing out. Good riddance to bad rubbish. Now we'll be able to take over this town without interference.'

'Doc's going, too.' They watched the frail, blood-spitting Holliday, carpet bag in hand, sawn-off under arm, drift along to join them at the depot as the locomotive hissed steam, its engine idling. 'Who's them others with 'em?'

Behan spat a gob of tobacco juice and shaded his eyes against the sun. 'Looks like them three other cronies of theirs, Sherman McMasters, Texas Jack Vermilion and Turkey Creek Johnson. They must be shit-sceered of staying here without the Earps to protect them.'

The long stack of the locomotive began shooting black woodsmoke as the coffin was loaded in the guard's van; its bell clanged mournfully on the breeze, the rods of the big wheels churned and it slowly moved away. Doc was the last to swing aboard, looking around him with his shotgun raised, in his nervy manner.

'Well, I'll be a blue-assed baboon, they've finally gone.' The rumbustious Behan gave a bitter laugh. 'An' he's taken Josephine with him.' This latter fact cut deep and he snarled, 'I shoulda put a bullet in the back of his head. What wouldn't I give to see that man dead?'

'How much, exactly?'

'What?'

'Well, we bungled the job on him last night but it can still be done. How much is he worth dead?'

Sheriff Behan tugged at his drooping walrus moustache, dourly. 'How much did Ike give you?'

'Three hundred.'

'OK.' Behan spat baccy juice again. 'There'll be another three hundred when you get back. But this time make sure of him.'

'No problem.' Stillwell strode inside the office, took his carbine from the rack. 'The stage for Tucson's just leaving. They allus give the railroad a race for their money. Don't worry. Earp ain't gonna get away scot free, not this time.'

He ran across and jumped up on to the box of the Wells Fargo stage as the driver cracked his whip over the backs of the six horses. 'Room for one more?' he asked, as it went racing out of town.

When they reached Tucson, Wyatt arranged for his family to stay the night with the others in the town hotel. They would be putting Morgan's body on the train for California which would be pulling out the next morning. After they had eaten, Wyatt said to Doc, Warren and Texas Jack, 'Fancy taking a walk along to the railyards?'

The comely Josephine, in her travelling costume, looked startled. 'What's wrong, Wyatt?'

'Nothing.' Earp checked his revolver picked up his shotgun, and nodded to Doc. 'We're just going to make sure they transfer the coffin.'

It was dark by the time they reached the yards. 'You got a feeling we're being followed?' Doc hissed out.

'Yeah,' Wyatt muttered, thumbing the hammers of his double-barrel. 'You two go on to the office.' They could see the lantern light in the distance. 'I'll see who it is.'

He dodged behind a box car in the sidings and rolled underneath the wheels to the other side of the rails, then watched as the crunch of boots on gravel approached from the far side. When whoever it was had passed, Wyatt rolled back under the car, got to his feet and saw the dark shape of some *hombre* heading after the other two. He had a revolver swinging from his fist.

Wyatt darted forward and stuck the shotgun in his back. 'OK, drop it, mister. Grab air if you know what's good for you.'

The man froze and reluctantly tossed the revolver away, turning to meet Earp's eyes.

'Stillwell, I mighta guessed. Mister, you're under arrest for the murder of my brother.'

Stillwell made a sudden grab for the shotgun barrel, trying to wrestle it away and turn it on Earp. He was a strong, middle-aged man and for moments it was anybody's guess which way the struggle would go. But, gradually Wyatt's anger and superior strength forced the weapon down until the right-hand barrel was just beneath the deputy's heart. He squeezed the trigger of the first barrel and that of the second for good measure. 'Aagh!' Stillwell screamed out, as he was bowled backwards by the buckshot. He lay there bleeding but still breathing as the others ran back.

He would not have lived for long, but Warren, Doc and Texas Jack all put slugs in him to make sure. 'That's for Morgan,' Warren whispered, his emptied gun smoking.

'Yeah,' Doc coughed out, his hand to his frail chest as the pungent gunsmoke rolled. 'That's one snake who deserved to die.'

Lucy looked radiant in a white dress and a mantilla of lace as she was driven in a hired buggy to the little whitewashed Spanish church on the edge of River Bend. Tim, who had bought himself a grey tweed suit for the occasion, was waiting for her at the door with Chico.

Her father, her uncle Walt, Aunt Nell, and a couple of cousins, had arrived on the stage from Tombstone, and Lucy's two younger sisters were adorned in blue, flowers in their hair, as her bridesmaids. There was hardly room for them all to pack into the small space along with some other town well-wishers.

The disaster at the mine, Manuel still being in a bad way, and the news that Morgan Earp had been killed, had cast a shadow over the proceedings, but they had agreed that the wedding should go on. Lucy's father and Tim, although opposite types, appeared to get on straight away, she was pleased to note. Yes, she was more than happy to be standing there by Tim's side as the priest intoned Latin words and pronounced them man and wife. Then their lips met passionately as the cowboy grabbed his gal in a strong embrace.

With a flourish of his sombrero, Chico was not slow to kiss the bride and bridesmaids, too, until Dolly grabbed hold of his elbow and told him to simmer down.

'Hey,' he cried, with a shrug. 'I am just happy for my friend, thassall. You don' theenk I—?'

'Yes, I do. You keep your greasy fingers off them two sisters. They're only sixteen.'

'No, I'm fifteen,' Violet butted in, smiling sweetly as she held her bouquet. 'You gonna dance with me, Chico?'

'No, he ain't,' Dolly said. 'He's gonna behave himself.'

'Who's she?' Violet asked. 'Chico's mother'.'

If looks could kill, Darling Dolly's would have made Violet wilt.

'No, she's his lover,' Lucy hissed in her ear. 'So don't you go causing trouble.'

Dolly had invited them all back to a reception in the Silver Cartwheel. She had spared no expense in laying on hams, joints of beef, sweet potatoes, pies, jellies, peaches and cream, and a superb wedding cake. The table virtually groaned. Wine, liquor and champagne flowed as the bride cut the cake and toasts were made.

'Who has paid for all this?' Chico asked.

'Lance, although he don't know it,' Dolly smiled. 'While the boss is away the mice will play.'

The professor of ivories had begun to jangle the keys accompanied by a squeezebox artist and a fiddler. Uncle Walt had jumped on a table and was singing out, *'Meet your partners and all chaw hay, dozee doh and take her away.'*

The floor was cleared for a square dance, the roulette table shoved to one side. The leather-lunged Walt was stomping the table and crooning, *'Birdie hop out and crane hop in, three hands round and go it again.'*

Chico and Violet led the reel – for Dolly had gone off to get in more liquor – sashaying up and swinging each other lustily around as the line-up on each side whooped and clapped to the beat. Everybody was having a fine old time as only settlers on the frontier knew how. Work hard and play hard was their maxim.

'I sure am sorry I can't get out there with you, honey,' Tim said, as he sat with his arm around Lucy, 'but I could only hop around like a crazy bird with this leg the way it is. Why don't you dance?'

'No,' she murmured, 'if it's not with you it won't be with anybody.'

*

'My daddy give me this watch. See, it's got, "To Ike, best wishes on your 21st, the Old Man". Solid gold it is. The only thang in this world I value.' Clanton was in a maudlin mood as he swung the hunter, big as an onion, by its gold chain. 'But the dang thang don't work.'

Lance shrugged. 'Take it into a watchmaker's when you're in town. Might just need a clean.'

'Aw, I ain't got time for that kinda shit.' Ike fixed the chain to an eye of his soup-stained waistcoat, tucked it in a pocket and growled, 'So, what is it you want with us, mister?'

'You've had a thousand of my cash up front. Regard that as a down payment. I'll make you a partner in my mine – when it's mine.'

'What kinda partner?'

'Fifty-fifty.'

'You joking? I'll need seventy per cent of the profits.' Ike scratched at the neck of his grubby, collarless shirt and tried to snatch at a fly. 'Remember I got overheads. I gotta pay my boys.'

'Sixty-forty, maybe. We can set their wages aside out of the profits. For Chris'sakes, Ike, don't you understand? This is big. There could be a million for us in this. I'm not sitting here haggling all day.'

'A million, huh?' Clanton's whiskey-befuddled mind considered this as he sprawled in the kitchen chair at Pete Spence's ranch. 'OK, it's a deal. We'll draw up a proper legal document. Partners in this mine, 60-40 to me.'

Pete Spence clattered into the kitchen in his ranch leathers and booted spurs, carrying a carbine. 'What's going on, Ike?'

'Pete, we're gonna help this bozo out. Once we git his mine churning out silver there'll be a good bonus in this for you and the boys.'

'What sort of bonus?'

Ike gave a grimace. 'A thousand, maybe. Only you'll have to wait for it.'

'And I'll have to get hold of the mine first,' Lance declared, impatient with these dunderheads.

'So,' Abe asked, 'what do you want us to do?'

'Take over River Bend and dispose of two – no three – troublemakers. One's a girl. Once they're out of the way the mine's ours.'

'So,' Pete Spence yelled, 'what we waitin' fer? Let's ride.'

Apart from the snappy dude, Johnny Ringo, in his black and silver rig, the rest of the twenty-strong gang were as dirty, greasy and uncouth as any prairie rat likely to be encountered on the frontier. All strung with bullets and iron, they leaped on their half-wild mustangs and set off behind Ike Clanton through a rugged land of turret buttes and salt canyons for years the stronghold of the great warriors Cochise and his nephew Geronimo. But now the white men were the masters after a long and bitter war.

They reached the San Pedro and watered their horses at Bisbee, quenching their own thirsts in the saloons as the afternoon sun beat down. Much to the relief of the citizenry, after the *siesta* they rode on.

It was sundown by the time they reached River Bend and hauled in outside the Silver Cartwheel. 'What'n hell's all that caterwauling?' Lance was surprised to hear the sound of fiddles, guitars, dancing and merriment coming from the open windows and doors of the saloon. 'What's going on?'

'Sounds like somebody's having a party,' Johnny Ringo grinned, spinning his silver-engraved revolver on his finger and firing some shots in the air. 'Let's join in, boys.'

'Hold it,' Lance shouted. 'I'll handle this. You guys just back me up.'

When he pushed through the batwing doors with Ike Clanton and Ringo beside him the wedding celebrations slowly wound to a halt as Tim struggled to his feet leaning on his crutch, Lucy supporting him. Dolly, in her new dress and hat, stared at them with surprise.

'Lance?' she cried. 'You're back. What are you doing here?'

'I might ask you, and this tribe, that question. This happens to be my saloon.'

'I thought you'd gone. I've been running things

137

for you,' Dolly said. 'Lance, please don't cause any trouble; this is Lucy's wedding day.'

'It is, is it? Who said you could hold a private shindig in my saloon?' He picked up a half-empty bottle of champagne and took a swig, wiping his mouth with a gloved hand. 'You ain't been stinting yourselves, I see.'

'Young man, I'm quite willing to pay for all the hospitality we've had.' Lucy's father stood up and faced him. 'Only we were told it was on the house.'

'You were, were you. So who might you be?'

'The bride's father.' He fished out a card from his coat pocket and offered it. 'I operate out of Tombstone.'

'You do, do you? Well, you better hurry back there unless you want us to erect one here for you.'

'There's no need for that talk,' Tim Roberts said. 'We assumed you were dead or gone for good. But it looks like a bad penny allus turns up again. I see you got another gang of bully boys with you to do your dirty work. Well, all these people here are respectable citizens and we ain't gonna be intimidated by the likes of you.'

'You ain't, ain't you?' Lance smiled. 'We'll see about that.'

'*Sí*, an' we might see about it, too,' Chico put in. 'How about you an' me deciding this ourselves, Patterson?' He loosened the clip of his holster and patted the butt of his old Navy Colt. 'Or is a murderer like you too yellow to meet a man face to face?'

'Who's the fancy-dress greaseball?' Clanton growled. 'He fancies his chances, don't he? I got twenty men outside, Mex. You gonna fight us all?'

'Please, don't let's have bloodshed on my daughter's wedding day.' Lucy's father held up his hands. 'Haven't you caused enough trouble in Tombstone, Clanton, without causing more down here?'

'My middle name's trouble,' Ike cackled. 'You think I give a monkey's fart for you, storekeeper? You better keep out of this and hurry back home to put your apron on.'

Tim hobbled forward, putting his free arm out across his father-in-law. 'Maybe you and your relations better do what he says, get the next stage outa here. And take Lucy with you. Chico, keep out of it.' He eyed several of the desperadoes who had pushed into the saloon behind Clanton. 'The odds aren't worth it.'

Dolly suddenly ran up to Lance and screamed out, 'What is it you want? Why don't you leave us alone?'

For answer Lance backhanded her across the jaw and she went sprawling to the floor. 'Shut up, you two-timing slut.'

Tim held Chico back. 'State your terms, Lance. What is it you want?'

'Just a minute. You other folks, get outa here.

You, too, mister,' he ordered Lucy's father. 'There should be a stage pulling out at 10 p.m. I want you all on it. Go on, blow.'

'Dad, do as he says,' Lucy called. 'You're not a gunfighter. Tim and I can handle this.'

'No, I—'

'Go on, get out.' Some of the thugs stepped forward and rounded up the wedding guests and musicians, prodding them with their carbines and revolvers towards the door, laughing and jeering as they herded them out.

When they had gone Patterson smiled. 'All I want is that mine. I'll pay you a hundred dollars for it, so it's all nice and legal. I'll give you tonight to think it over. You two'll meet me at Lawyer Higgins's office at ten in the morning and sign over the deeds to me. Is that understood?'

'A hundred dollars?' Tim scoffed. 'You're joking.'

'It's daylight robbery,' Lucy said. 'Come on, Tim, we'll think about it.'

'You better think pretty hard, missy,' Clanton roared. 'You know that offer makes sense. Otherwise me an' my boys are gonna come looking for you.'

Chico helped Dolly to her feet and thrust his way past Johnny Ringo, '*Vayamos, muchacha*, you better come with me.'

'Yeah, take the old bat,' Lance sneered. 'Meanwhile I'll be totting up how much you owe me for this shindig.'

'It's all in the account books,' Dolly called back, tossing her scarf around her throat. 'We just gave ourselves a li'l raise, thassall.'

'Hey, greaser,' Ringo called, flashing his smile, 'I'll be looking for you.'

'Eef you do you better be sayin' your prayers.' Chico grinned and shrugged and followed his friends out, hurrying to catch up with the wedding guests.

Before they all clambered into and up on top of the stage Lucy's father made her promise that she would sign over the mine. 'You come back and work in the store. We'll find Tim a job, too. It's no use fighting these sort of people, Lucy. Look what happened to the the Earps. You promise me you'll sell that mine and come home.'

'Yes, I promise,' she called. 'We'll see you in Tombstone.'

'Did you mean that?' Tim asked, as they stood and watched the stage rumble away into the night. 'I guess it's good advice.'

'I don't know, Tim. Why should we give up our mine to those murderers? Why should we be pushed around? Can't we send for the army?'

'It's too late for that.' Tim looked worried as he put an arm around her. 'Let's go back to the ranch. Who knows what tomorrow will bring.'

As Chico drove the buggy away, Clanton's hooligans had already begun hurrahing the town, shooting off their guns, riding up and down, smashing windows, yelling, drinking and generally making a nuisance of themselves.

'Eet is goin' to be noisy for the citizens tonight,' Chico laughed. 'Why they not bring fireworks? Go whole hog!'

Lucy bit her lip as she hung on to Tim's arm. 'Yes,' she said, 'I doubt if the illustrious Sheriff McBean will be keeping much order. I only hope nobody gets killed.'

TEN

'What a way to spend my first wedding night.' Tim Roberts pulled on his Levi jeans in the candlelight and grinned at Lucy. It was two in the morning. 'I gotta go take over from Chico.'

He stepped out into the chill moonlight where his Mexican friend had been keeping guard for four hours. 'Any sign of anybody?' They had feared the whiskied-up gang might take it into their heads to attack in the night and burn the house down.

Chico shook his head. 'You gonna surrender the mine to those murderin' lice?'

'I guess so.' Tim pulled up the collar of his jacket. 'If it was just you and me, buddy, we'd burn their whiskers with some lead then head outa here fast. But I got Lucy to think of. I can't just hightail it and leave her. I got responsibilities. They are desperate men who will stop at nothing to get what they want.'

143

Chico could sense his fear. He was not immune to it himself. Who would not know fear and shame against such odds, two once-carefree *caballeros* against that pack of *renegados*?

He shivered, pulling his poncho around him. 'It cold. I go get Dolly to make me warm.'

'Yeah.' When he had gone in Tim went over to the barn and settled himself in a corn crib. The hay was mighty comfortable. He was going to have difficulty staying awake. All was quiet but for the shrill wails of the coyotes. A half-moon rode high amid a myriad of shooting stars. It reminded him of those nights when they awaited the terror of Apache attacks. Yes, all men knew fear. The challenge was to stay calm and conquer it. Perhaps the worst fear was the thought of being branded a coward.

'What you going to do if they don't show?' Ike Clanton's whiskey-hoarse question was aimed at Lance Patterson, who was at the bar taking his early morning Irish coffee. 'You wan' us to smoke the rats out of their hole?'

Lance nodded. 'If they accept my offer they can live and go about their business. It's the only sensible thing for them to do. But if they don't,' he drew his thumb across his throat and made a croaking sound, 'it's the end for them.'

Clanton scratched at his hairy chest, pursuing lice. He only bathed once a year. He figured it weakened a man. The other desperadoes were sprawled around the saloon, on chairs or laid out on the floor, coming round at the sound of voices, groaning and holding their heads after the night's rutting and roistering. Ike's brother, Phin, was still upstairs snoring in the arms of the Peruvian Paula.

'Get off me, you pig,' she suddenly snorted, pushing him from the narrow bunk to land with a thump on the floorboards, making the candelabra beneath wobble wildly.

'What's the matter with you?' Phin shouted. 'Wake up, you whore. I'm gonna give you another seein'-to.'

'Buckle on your guns, boys,' Ike shouted. 'Gargle your breakfast coffin varnish at the bar. But only a couple. We might well have some varmints to shoot. Christ, your eyes, Bill! They look like red coals gleaming outa hell.'

'You should see 'em from my side,' Curly Bill Brocius moaned as he lurched to the bar and clutched a bottle.

Lance Patterson went out on to the sidewalk and watched the town awakening, storekeepers opening up, small-time farmers arriving on their wagons with produce for the open market, Mexicans on burros going out to their stony fields, and a bustle of packrat miners coming out of the boarding-houses to load up their mules with pick-axes and buckets. News of Crazy Ned's mine had spread fast and the panhandlers had been quick to arrive to search around the hills in the vicinity. So far none of the hopefuls had struck a seam of silver like Ned's.

Lance almost salivated at the thought of the riches awaiting him. But he would have to move fast. This time, with Clanton and his fast-shooters behind him, there would be no argument. He heard the horn halloo announcing the arrival of the early morning stage from Bisbee. A couple of ranchers and their wives stepped down, and a gent in a white canvas suit and fedora hat, who collected a carpet bag from the boot.

'Who's that bozo?' Lance muttered, as the stage driver pointed him on his way down the street.

Suddenly he saw Lucy Roberts, in her Stetson, neat blouse, leather riding skirt and boots, drive her wagon into town. She pulled in outside the lawyer's office and helped Tim Roberts climb down. Then they went into Higgins's office.

'So they've caved in?' A smile spread over Patterson's face. He consulted his watch. 'Why they so early? I'll get my coat and gun and go along.'

The man in the white canvas suit, Frank McMasters, entered Higgins's office in time to overhear Lucy explaining to the little bald-headed attorney that she and Tim wanted to draw up documents for the sale of their Latigo Canyon Mine.

'We're in rather a hurry,' she said. 'I want to

146

catch the stage to Bisbee. I'd be glad if you'd expedite things.'

'Who you selling to?' Higgins asked, opening a file.

'Lance Patterson, the saloon-keeper. He'll be along shortly.'

'How much you asking?'

'A hundred,' she said, with a resigned sigh.

'Excuse me,' McMasters butted in. 'Are you the legal owners of that mine.'

'That's right. Why?'

'May I introduce myself. Frank McMasters.' He offered his hand to the girl. 'I'm a mining engineer. Boss of Tombstone Incorporated Holdings. My men have already taken a look at your mine while you were away. That is first grade ore. Did I hear you correctly? You're letting it go for a hundred thousand?'

Tim had a fit of coughing and squeezed his wife's knee beneath the table. 'A hundred *thousand*?' He winked at her. 'That's what Lance offered, ain't it?'

McMasters pounced. 'I'll up the offer to a hundred and twenty. Get those documents ready to sign, Mr Higgins.'

'What about Lance?' Lucy gave Tim a worried look.

'He's been outbid,' Tim drawled. 'I'll tell him so, myself.'

*

Lance Patterson was striding down the street towards the lawyer's office when the coach to Bisbee passed him. He saw Tim Roberts wave it to a halt with his crutch. Before Lucy climbed aboard she waved a piece of paper his way.

'What's going on?' Patterson shouted, angrily.

Roberts stood facing him. 'It's just you and me now, Lance.'

'What?' Patterson stopped in his tracks fifty paces away. 'Are you going to sign that mine over to me or—'

'We've had a better offer, Lance. Not your measly one hundred. One hundred and twenty thousand. Lucy's just off to pay the banker's cheque into Wells Fargo bank at Bisbee.'

'You double-crossing. . . .' Lance's right hand slid towards the walnut butt of the Remington stuffed into his belt, but his words faltered, 'You lousy polecats.'

The slim young cowboy rested with his crutch beneath his left arm as his right hand, too, snaked towards the low-thonged Peacemaker strapped over his denims. 'Yep, go for it, Lance. I bet you didn't hesitate before you gunned down Crazy Ned.'

'Why, you cream-puff cow-poke. You ain't got a chance in hell of living through this. I'll show you.' Lance backed away, then turned and started to run towards the saloon as Ike Clanton and some of his boys stumbled out on to the sidewalk.

'Kill him,' Lance screamed.

Ike grinned and stood there, arms akimbo. 'Looks like it's down to you, saloon-keep.'

'No, please, I'll pay you,' Lance pleaded. 'You can have the whole share.'

Lance yelped as a bullet from the grinning Ringo bit off his earlobe. As blood dripped he knew he was going to get no help from Clanton. Stealthily, he drew his heavy Remington and spun around, blamming away immediately at Roberts who was hobbling awkwardly towards him.

Tim Roberts was one of those men who knew that successful gunfighting was based on his taking his time. He took his stand, mentally unflustered, as the lead scattered at him by the panicked Patterson whipped and whined past his head. His arm muscle snapped into action, the Peacemaker was in his grip. He cocked and aimed it with calm deliberateness, his arm extended, taking aim. The barrel barked flame and lead and Patterson's false cockiness came to an end. He went spinning on to his back in the dust, his shirt-front flowering blood. He tried to fire again, but Tim finished him with two more slugs and he fell back lifeless.

It was only then that Ike and his men started firing. Tim's crock leg forbade fast movement so all he could do was stand there and face the fusillade as he spent his last three bullets. So, this is it, he thought, grimly. The big goodbye. Just when—

But suddenly the rustlers were distracted by the

arrival of four dark-clothed avengers who galloped down the street and whirled their mustangs in a cloud of dust before the saloon. 'How about trying us, Clanton?' Wyatt Earp yelled.

Clanton quickly dodged back into the saloon, tumbling through the batwing doors. But Curly Bill Brocius stood there gaping. 'Where'n hell you come from?'

'That's where you're going,' Wyatt shouted, and, with similar coolness as Tim's under fire, raised his shotgun and blasted Curly into eternity.

Wyatt, Warren, Doc and Bat had been sworn in at Tucson as US Marshals and were bent on revenge for Morgan's death. Their first target had been Pete Spence's ranch, but as they approached along a canyon they had come face to face with Indian Charlie. They halted their horses as Wyatt called out, 'We want you, Charlie, for the murder of Morgan.'

'It weren't just me,' Indian Charlie had pleaded. 'They give me twenty-five dollars. I just—'

'Twenty-five dollars for my brother's life!' The words incensed Wyatt and he gritted out, 'Do you want to hang, you rat, or—?'

Indian Charlie went for his gun but in his fear fumbled the shot. Wyatt's lead cut him down. Before he choked on his blood, Indian Charlie told them where Clanton and his boys had gone. That's how Wyatt and the three other marshals arrived in River Bend. Four crack shots, the Earps,

Doc Holliday and Bat Masterson. Four aces!

But things were hotting up. They had to leap from their mustangs and take cover as lead was blasted their way by the men outside the saloon. Others had smashed the windows and were firing from inside. All was bedlam.

Inside the saloon, Ike urged his boys on. 'Keep shootin',' he shouted. 'We've got 'em pinned down.' But his murky eyes met those of Hank Swilling and he jerked his head towards the bar. 'This looks bad, Hank,' he growled, as he stuffed a couple of bottles of whiskey in his coat pockets. 'I'm getting out.'

They both skedaddled out of the saloon back door and found their mounts in the stables. They saddled up hurriedly and went galloping away out of the back of the town, swinging away south towards the border, heading straight as an arrow across the plains towards the hills.

Pete Spence had seen them leave and followed them out. He watched them go, then grabbed his own horse and started off north along the San Pedro back to Tombstone.

Johnny Ringo decided to make a break for freedom, too, but his horse was out front. He edged away along the sidewalk, shooting as he went. Bat cut him down with a heart shot.

Pony Deal, too, thought he could shoot his way out. He made a run across the street but Tim's blazing sixguns toppled him.

Otherwise, out in front of the saloon, as their leaders fled, the battle still raged. Like a pack of cornered wolves those still alive had no intention of surrendering.

'How we gonna smoke 'em out?' Doc called, as he reloaded his revolver. 'I'm running outa slugs.'

Phin Clanton had tumbled out of bed at the sound of the shooting and craftily edged his rifle out of the bedroom window. He didn't have a good view of the four attackers but he was waiting his chance. 'Ahh,' he breathed as he got Warren Earp in his sights and took first squeeze of the trigger.

Suddenly there was a shrill hallooing as Chico Chavez, in his big sombrero, came galloping Satan down the street. He was waving two sticks of dynamite in his hand. He reared Satan up on his back hoofs and hurled them through the saloon door.

Ker-rumpf! There was a moment of silence as Chico hared away. Then the dynamite exploded, blowing the saloon to smithereens. The bodies of men came flying through the air amid a shower of splintered walls and furniture, blood-splattered remains of the less fortunate hitting the dust.

Tim watched a bloody head roll towards him and gritted out, 'Trust Chico to overdo things.'

Lucy had stopped the stage outside town and came running back. She threw her arms around Tim's waist as he stood there with his smoking gun. 'Are you OK?'

'Sure,' he grinned, hugging and kissing her. 'It

looks like we've won.'

Dolly had gone up the back stairs of the saloon and ushered the girls out before Chico made his charge along the street.

'My hero,' she cried, as he came galloping back. 'You saved the day, but you sure made a mess of the Silver Cartwheel.'

'Lance won't be needing it no more,' Tim said, looking around at the fallen bodies. 'I guess we got some burying to do.'

'An' some hanging.' A big, bearded farmer had led a party of citizens, all buzzing with fury at the way the town had been shot up, to harangue Sheriff McBean, who had arrived on the scene somewhat belatedly. 'We want all them *bandidos* who're still alive strung up. It's time we made use of our gallows. Come on, Sheriff, shake your bones or you'll be out of your job.'

'You cain't just hang them that's wounded,' McBean protested.

'So, git the doc to patch 'em up, put 'em before the judge in the marnin',' the big man said, 'and we'll hang 'em at noon.'

'You hear that, McBean? People have had enough of outlawry.' Wyatt, in his dusty frock coat, strode across and smiled at Lucy. 'Sorry I couldn't git to your wedding, gal, but I been kinda busy.'

'That's OK, Wyatt,' Lucy cried. 'You've given me my best wedding present. You saved my husband's life.'

'Yeah.' Tim stuck out his hand to shake. 'I'd like to thank you, Marshal.'

'My work ain't over yet. The valleys around Tombstone are still crawling with killers. It's time to flush 'em all out.' His strong grip crushed the cowboy's hand. 'You struck me as a good shot and a brave man, Tim. You care to join us?'

'No, I'll leave that work to you, Marshal.' Tim put his arm around Lucy's waist. 'We got important things to do, like maybe buy some more land along the San Pedro, build up a herd, hire some hands and improve the ranch house.'

'And,' Lucy smiled, 'start a family. We're gonna be real busy, Wyatt, but you call in an' see us any time.'

They waved goodbye as the two Earp brothers, Doc Holliday and Bat Masterson holstered their weapons, mounted up and rode out of town towards the border to search for Ike Clanton. Soon they were just four dark figures on horseback lost in a shimmering heat-haze.

So, in the weeks that followed, after the citizens had had their hangings, life became more peaceful around River Bend. Tim and Lucy were busy buying stock and extending their holdings along the river. Darling Dolly, with the cash she had purloined from Lance's safe, had rebuilt the Silver Cartwheel and presided as the new boss of the establishment. Life looked rosy. The River Bend citizens' committee had kicked out McBean and elected Tom Archer, who had made a good recovery, as sheriff. Manuel was in a wheelchair, but made himself useful, at a good wage, in the Roberts's saddlery.

The death of Morgan had affected Wyatt deeply. For several months his quest for vengeance did not falter as he and his posse scoured the border canyons. Everywhere they rode in Cochise County the outlaws and rustlers fled. Word was out that it was death to be caught by the Four Aces.

However, they never did catch Ike Clanton and his sidekick, Swilling, who had disappeared into Mexico. Pete Spence, too, had placed himself under the protection of Sheriff Behan and was skulking in his jail until the trouble blew over.

One day Chico came racing into the Roberts's ranch on Satan looking as if the hounds of hell were after him.

'What you been up to, *hombre*?' Tim called. 'You robbed the bank or something?'

Chico wheeled Satan, a worried look on his face. 'No, I just called in to say goodbye. Dolly's after me. She wants to get married. I just remember I got a sick mama I got to see in Mexico. *Adios, muchachas.*'

He set off across the plains towards the border and freedom and was just a plume of dust in the distance as Dolly hared into the ranch on her new buggy. She, too, peered after the fast disappearing Chico.

'That dad-blasted Mexican,' she wailed. 'I mighta known.'

A year later Lucy was standing at the ranch house door watching the sunset, a baby in her arms, when she saw Tim returning from the range. There was a Mexican in a big sombrero on a feisty stallion loping along by his side.

'Dolly,' she called to the saloon-owner who was visiting and helping prepare supper. 'We've got a visitor.'

Dolly joined her to stare out into the red sunset glow at the two dark silhouettes approaching. 'Is it?' She blinked back tears. 'Can it be?'

'Yes, it is.'

'That bastard!' She started off running towards the riders. 'I'll kill him!' she screamed.

Lucy smiled as she saw Chico bend down and swoop Darling Dolly to sit on his lap across his saddle. She was hugging and kissing him when they rode in. 'Those Mexican *señoritas*,' Chico said, with a flashing grin, 'they OK, but I mees havin' a real woman. I guess it time I marry, huh?'

Dolly grinned as she hung on to him. 'You ain't gettin' out of it this time.'

It was a more than convivial evening and after supper Chico pulled out a big gold watch and swung it by its chain. 'Guess who thees belong to?'

Tim took it, flicked it open, read the inscription, and muttered, 'Ike Clanton.'

'*Sí*, I bump into him along the Rio Grande at El Plomo. He try to cheat me at cards. I had to shoot the sonuvbitch. But don't let it get around,' he smiled. 'I don' wan' to get a bad reputation. His damn watch don't work, anyway.'

That only made them laugh the more. Even baby Charlie chuckled. It was good to have Chico back.

AFTERWORD

Forty million dollars in silver and three million in gold was yielded by the mines around Tombstone and its environs. The mines became flooded in the 1890s, were abandoned and Tombstone became a ghost town. Today it has been restored as a tourist attraction.

Wyatt eventually hung up his guns and made a small fortune in California speculating in oil, copper and gold. When his wife, Mattie, died, he married his young mistress, Josephine. He died in 1929, aged 80. Josephine died in 1944 at the age of 83. There were no children.

His great friend, Doc Holliday, died in a sanatorium in Colorado of tuberculosis. He was 36. Bat Masterson became a sports writer in New York and died at his desk in 1921. He once commented, 'We didn't kill as many men as they say we did.' He himself was credited with thirty-five fatal shootings.